THE GHOST OF
LOST ISLAND

THE GHOST OF LOST ISLAND

~·~·~·~·~·~·~·~·~·~·~·~·~·~·~·~·~·~

Liza Ketchum Murrow

Holiday House / New York

For Pete, Marty, Cora, and Silas Hagerty,
with thanks for sharing the island
—and its ghost—with me

The lines from the song on pages 77 and 162 are from "Delia's Gone," words and music by Blind Blake. TRO—© Copyright 1952 (renewed) 1954 (renewed) Hollis Music, Inc., New York, N.Y. Used by permission.

Library of Congress Cataloging-in-Publication Data
Murrow, Liza Ketchum
The ghost of Lost Island / by Liza Ketchum Murrow. —1st ed.
p.   cm.
Summary: While helping his grandfather herd and shear his flock of sheep on a small island off the coast of Maine, twelve-year-old Gabe encounters a mysterious woman who may be the ghost of a drowned milkmaid.
ISBN 0-8234-0874-4
[1. Islands—Fiction.   2. Ghosts—Fiction.   3. Sheep—Fiction.
4. Grandfathers—Fiction.   5. Maine—Fiction.   6. Mystery and detective stories.]   I. Title.
PZ7.M96713Gh   1991
[Fic]—dc20   90-47671   CIP   AC

Contents

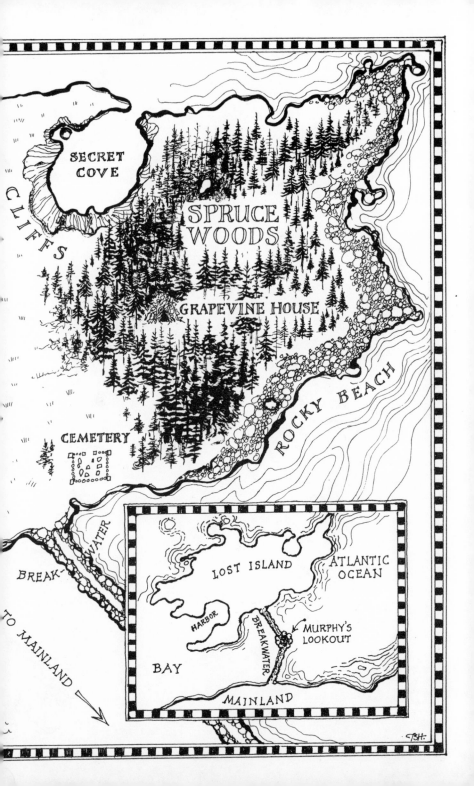

Author's Note

Sheep have grazed on the islands off the Maine coast since colonial times. By the beginning of this century, the practice had died out, but in recent years landowners have brought sheep back to a number of islands. The sheep keep the island pastures open, and they can survive without extra hay or grain, as long as the winters aren't too harsh. They are usually rugged breeds, used to foraging for their food (some even learn to eat seaweed); they take shelter in wooded areas during bad weather and don't require much attention except at shearing time or in late spring, when their lambs are born.

If the island is near the mainland, the sheep farmer can move his sheep by walking or swimming them out when the moon creates an extra low tide.

When the island is farther away, the sheep are moved in boats.

Many sheep farmers use Border collies to round up the animals, move them from one part of the island to another, or separate a few sheep from the rest of the flock. Border collies are medium-sized, black-and-white dogs who are specially trained to work with sheep.

The island in this story is imaginary, as are all the characters, but "Lost Island" is typical of islands up and down the Maine coast where an old tradition has been revived.

A number of friends and family members have helped with this book. Thanks to my husband, Casey Murrow, and to Peter Shiras, for assistance with boats, machinery, and tides; to Margery Cuyler, for her supportive and imaginative editing; and to Eileen Christelow, Karen Hesse, Katherine Leiner, and Bob MacLean for their insightful comments. Three fine shepherds—Pete Hagerty, Andy Rice, and my mother, Barbara Ketchum—have been generous with their knowledge of sheep ever since we started our own small flock. I am very grateful for their advice and suggestions about the imaginary sheep on "Lost Island."

THE GHOST OF LOST ISLAND

1

Ghost Island

The day before the shearing, Grandfather took me out to the island to spend the night. Uncle Paul and my sister Ginny helped us load the boat while MacDuff, Grandfather's Border collie, ran around our legs trying to herd us.

"Don't worry, Duffer," I said, scratching MacDuff's neck, "we won't leave you behind. We can't round up the sheep without you."

Grandfather's been keeping sheep on Lost Island for three years, but this was my first time out to help with the shearing. Ginny's already been twice, even though she's only a year older.

"It's just because she's big for her age," my dad said last year, when I complained about staying behind.

It's true, Ginny's tall and wiry, but that's not the

3

only reason Grandfather took her along. Ginny's not squeamish or clumsy the way I am, and Grandfather likes having her around when he's working with the sheep or building something.

Well, too bad for you, I thought, watching her hoist our heavy cooler out of the truck. This time, *I've* got Grandfather all to myself.

"Let's move the punt," Grandfather said.

The punt is Uncle Paul's boat; he uses it to get out to his lobster boat at its mooring. It has oars and a small outboard engine. Today it was in the tall grass at the top of the beach. We put driftwood logs under its belly to roll it down to the water.

"Heave-ho, mates," Grandfather grunted as we dug our boots into the sand. The outboard engine in the back made the punt heavy.

"Turned into a sea captain, Pop?" Uncle Paul teased.

Grandfather laughed. "I'm just a landlubber. You know I leave the boating and fishing to my boys— you and Gabriel." He wiped his forehead with an old handkerchief and put his hand on my shoulder. "With Gabriel here as my first mate, everything should be fine."

Ginny tossed her pigtail over her shoulder and rolled her eyes. "As long as you don't mind ending up in the bay," she said, low enough so only I could hear.

"At least I don't get seasick, like some people I know," I snapped back. That's the only way I get back at her. If she goes lobstering with Dad and Uncle Paul, she turns the color of tomalley—that's the green goop inside a lobster—and spends her whole time throwing up over the side. Dad says our family's divided into farmers and fishermen. With her stomach, Ginny will be a farmer, he says, and I'll end up on the water. "Unless he leans toward music, like me," my mom always adds.

"Hope you can make it through the night out there," my sister said now, as we pulled on the boat. "There's no electricity, you know."

"So what?" I answered, even though I'd never slept without my night-light before. Everyone else in sixth grade can probably sleep in the dark, but not me.

"Hey, you two, stop bickering," Uncle Paul said. "Pull on that line at the bow." We went to the front of the punt and tugged on the rope while the men shoved from behind. My boots slipped on the smooth stones near the water and I almost lost my grip.

"Watch out, Gabe!" Ginny scolded. "The boat's going to roll on you."

I managed to keep hold as we shoved the punt toward the surf. Before Ginny could tell me what to do next, I jumped in and bailed the boat with a plastic milk jug. When her back was turned, I threw some water on her jacket.

"Jerk!" she yelled. "Grandfather, look what Gabe did!"

Grandfather frowned. "We haven't got time for that now, Gabriel. Let's load up."

I helped him stuff our bags of clothes and the cooler full of food up in the bow. Grandfather stowed his metal sheep's crook, some tools, and a box of nails under the seat.

"Gabe, aren't you forgetting something?" Ginny called in her know-it-all voice. She held up my orange life jacket.

"Shut up," I hissed, but I put it on. Boy, was it nice to be getting away from her for a few days. Ever since she turned thirteen and started wearing a bra and braces, she's ordered me around like a drill sergeant. My mom says girls always shoot up faster than boys, and it will even out in the end, but I wish I could stretch myself up six or seven inches right now. My little private song about Ginny went round and round in my head: *Older sisters are a pain, I'd like to flush them down the drain.*

"Come along, my Duffer." Grandfather always makes it sound like singing when he talks to his dog. MacDuff put his tail between his legs and whined. He was afraid of the boat.

"Right *here* now," Grandfather commanded,

pointing at his rubber boots. MacDuff scrambled into the punt and curled up next to Grandfather's feet.

Uncle Paul put his heavy hand on my arm. "Here's a little present—in case you feel like reading under the covers." He gave me a black flashlight, the kind that shines a long way even though it's tiny. "Thanks, Uncle Paul," I said. I tried it out, then put it in my jacket pocket. Now I wouldn't have to be afraid of the dark.

I stepped into the stern and sat facing Grandfather. The boat rolled from side to side as Grandfather slipped the oars into the oarlocks.

"Aren't you going to use the engine, Pop?" Uncle Paul asked.

Grandfather shook his head. "Not on such a calm day. Anyway, you know I like the old ways—and it's a good chance for Gabriel to practice his rowing."

Uncle Paul snorted. "Whatever you say, Pop." He grinned at me, then flexed his arm, showing his muscle. "He just wants to build your strength, Gabriel."

I was disappointed. When Uncle Paul and I go fishing in the punt, he usually lets me run the engine when we're close to shore. Never mind, I thought. At least I'll be alone with Grandfather.

"Good luck," Ginny said, blowing a huge bubble with her gum so I couldn't see her face.

The boat rocked up and down. When the next wave broke, Uncle Paul pushed us out. "Have a good time!" The wind blew his cap off his head.

"Watch out for the ghost!" Ginny yelled.

"Be-wa-aare the dairymaid," Uncle Paul called in a quavery voice. The boat shot through the top of a wave, then banged down into the trough on the other side.

"Who's the dairymaid?" I shouted at Grandfather. He was straining over the oars.

"That's a story for later," Grandfather grunted. "When it's dark."

Another wave sprayed his shoulders and wet my face. "Is it a ghost story?" I asked.

He nodded. "Might scare you," he warned, winking at me.

"No it won't," I said. "I like ghosts." But of course I don't. Who does?

In a few minutes, we were in open water, rocking over the long swells. "All right, navigator," Grandfather said, "we want to head for the cove in the middle of the island."

I directed Grandfather as we inched slowly across the little bay. The island was long and low in the middle, rising to a high point at each end.

"It looks like a saddle," I said. "Why do they call it Lost Island?"

"I guess because it gets lost in the fog," Grandfather answered. "But it's only known as Lost Island on the charts. Folks who live here always call it Ghost Island."

I leaned toward him, sitting on my hands so I wouldn't bite my fingernails. "Will we really see a ghost?"

"If we're lucky." Grandfather's mouth turned up and I decided he was only teasing.

After a while we shifted seats so I could take the oars. I'd never rowed through such big swells. Sometimes we went in a zigzag line; I pulled too hard on the right side, or I hit the water with a flat oar, spraying us. Grandfather didn't seem to mind; he was looking at birds through his old binoculars.

"You'll get the hang of it before long," he said. "Pull on your port side now—we're a bit off course."

Pretty soon, I got us going straight. The rough wood of the oars burned my hands, but I bit my lip so Grandfather wouldn't think I was a wimp. From the middle of the bay, we could see the long curving breakwater connecting the island to the shore. Grandfather told me that people had built it years ago, to protect the bay from the ocean. In the middle, where the breakwater curved, was a big heap of stones; it looked like a giant's head with two rocky arms, one reaching out to sea, the other to land.

"Grandfather, what's that tower for?"

"It marks the breakwater, so boats remember it's there when the tide goes over the top. They call it Murphy's Lookout. Years ago, old Mr. Murphy used to perch up there looking for seals. Maybe that's what I'll do when I'm too old to farm."

I smiled at Grandfather. Even though he has white hair and a craggy face, he doesn't act like an old man. I took another long pull on the oars. "Can you walk all the way to the island on the breakwater?" I asked.

"Only at low tide. And it's risky."

We took turns rowing until we reached the island. Grandfather brought us into a tiny harbor where the water was calm and sent me up to the bow so I could jump out and pull the punt onto the beach. The surf splashed right into my boots. It was icy cold, but I didn't complain. I wanted to show Grandfather I knew what to do.

MacDuff leaped out and scurried through the tall beach grass. After Grandfather sank the anchor into the sand, we unloaded our bags into an old wheelbarrow with a hole in the bottom. Grandfather pushed it up a narrow path while I carried my backpack and a thermos of coffee.

There were droppings everywhere, even on the porch of the tiny cabin. "Where are the sheep?" I asked.

"All over the island," Grandfather said. "We'll find them after we get settled."

He unlocked the padlock on the door, and I followed him inside. The cabin was dark and musty. I stood in the middle of an open room while Grandfather used the claw on his hammer to pull nails from the window frames.

"We batten everything down in the winter," he said. "Storms can be fierce here. Push the windows open, can you?"

I turned the latches and banged the swollen frames until they swung out. Dead flies covered the windowsills. I looked around while Grandfather brought the cooler inside. A fat barrel stove sat in the middle of the room, next to a square table with rough benches.

"Here's where we sleep," Grandfather said. I followed him into a tiny bedroom with two sagging beds. "Hope you won't mind my snoring," he added.

"Where's the bathroom?" I asked.

He chuckled. "There's an outhouse down the trail. But since it's just us men, we can pee off the porch if we feel like it."

I ran outside. *Just us men*—Grandfather made me feel grown up. It was going to be great being here without my sister.

When I zipped up my pants, I noticed a tall white post with a crossbar dug into the ground.

"Grandfather—what's this ship's mast doing out here?"

"That's my flagpole," he said. "Come on, we'll run the flag up, show folks we're in residence." I heard a drawer open, then he came out with the Maine flag. I unfolded it, looking for the grommets, and we walked through the tall grass to the pole.

"Where's the rope?" I asked.

Grandfather was staring at the pole. He searched the ground at the base. "That's funny," he said, "I never take the rope down. Now who—" he glanced at me, cleared his throat, and said, "Never mind; we'll find a way to hoist it later."

We went back to the cabin, but I could tell he was still puzzling about it. He took off his cap and scratched his white hair until it stood up in fuzzy points. "I guess the ghost stole it," he said, winking at me.

I knew he was only kidding, but I looked around quickly. The island seemed lonesome, with the wind rippling through the grass and the ocean all around us. I hurried after him into the cabin.

2

The Grapevine
House

After lunch on the porch, we went beachcombing. Grandfather was looking for driftwood to repair the fences for the next day, when Uncle Paul and his friend Lenny would come out to help with the shearing. Grandfather showed me the secret cove on the west side of the island, where the best beach trash washes in. We made three trips with the wheelbarrow, hauling logs, wet boards, and even the mast from a small sailboat back to the field where we would shear the sheep.

When we had a big pile of wood scraps next to the pens, I held the boards steady while Grandfather drove the nails. "We'll make some movable panels to get the sheep where we want them. Sure is nice to have help," he said.

I was glad Ginny wasn't there to grab the hammer

and whiz in a nail, then tease me when mine went in crooked.

"This is the chute," Grandfather said as we stood the panels up on their sides, making two walls in the shape of a big V. "It's like a funnel," he explained. "We drive the sheep into the open end, then push them forward. When they get to the point of the V, we close the chute; from there we can push them one at a time through a gate into the holding pen."

The holding pen was a sturdy corral made of strong posts and lumber; Grandfather told me he and Uncle Paul had built it three years ago when they first brought sheep out to the island. Right next to it was a tiny pen just the right size for shearing one sheep at a time, and an open shed where Grandfather said we'd store the wool. We checked all the latches, and Grandfather let me grease the hinges and bolts so the gates would open easily.

After everything was ready, Grandfather decided to take a nap. He sat down in the tall grass, poured a cup of coffee from his thermos, and leaned back against a big boulder. "I'm going to catch forty winks," he said. "You go exploring." He waved his arm. "The whole island's your domain. Just stay away from the cliffs."

"You mean, I can go anywhere I want?" I asked.

"Why not? If you get lost, just climb to higher

ground, or listen for the ocean. You'll find your way back eventually. Take MacDuff; he knows every inch of the island." He pulled his cap down over his eyes.

Grandfather made me feel grown up, not like my mom and dad, who always want to know where I'm going and when I'll be back.

MacDuff and I crossed the big field. Sheep trails had packed down narrow paths, and sometimes we found little clumps of ewes, nibbling on the new spring grass. MacDuff's ears pricked up and he dropped to a crouch, waiting for my command. "Come here now," I called, trying to use Grand-father's singsongy voice. "You can work the sheep tomorrow."

At first, I kept looking back to make sure I didn't get lost. Then I climbed a tiny hill and looked around. Three lobster boats chugged beyond the breakwater, hauling traps. Ahead of me was a tangled patch of forest with dark and spooky trees. *Not* a good place to go, I decided. All kinds of creepy things could live in there. Then I thought of my sister. She'd never be afraid to explore the woods, especially in broad daylight. If only I could stop being such a coward.

I stood there a minute, trying to decide what to do, when MacDuff suddenly pricked up his ears and darted into the trees. "Hey, MacDuff—come back here!" I yelled. I took a few steps into the shadows. The white tip of his tail flickered under the spruce trees and then disappeared. "MacDuff!" I called again. The wind sighed through the grass all around me and then I heard MacDuff whimpering. Was he hurt? I took a deep breath and hurried after him, looking behind me a couple of times to make sure I knew how to get out.

I followed a narrow sheep trail winding between the trunks and prickly branches of the spruce trees. Pretty soon, the sun disappeared. Thin, pale-green moss coated the branches. I couldn't hear the wind, the sea, or the birds. I started walking more carefully, trying not to make noise. It seemed like an enchanted forest, where fairy tale characters were hiding.

I stopped for a minute and pulled a stick of gum from my pocket, pretending everything was normal. It's just a regular day, I told myself. You're out for a walk with the dog, chewing gum . . .

Suddenly, MacDuff yipped close by. I ran ahead. The path stopped in front of a rounded tangle of vines. They looked like the old grapevines at Grandfather's house, but instead of being trained into an arbor, they were bent and twisted like a tangled ball of string. MacDuff was sniffing the ground near a dark opening in the vines. He wagged his tail when he saw me, then disappeared into the underbrush.

"Duffer, you come back here!" I called. I peered into the shadows, but it was too dark to see anything. "MacDuff, are you there?"

I could hear him snuffling, but he wasn't growling, so it must be safe, right? Actually, I wasn't so sure, but I decided to go in. If I was going to learn to be brave, I might as well start now, when I had MacDuff to protect me. I took a deep breath and crawled through the opening.

The vines made a rounded shelter, tall enough for me to stand up in the middle, but low on the sides, like an igloo made of crisscrossed branches. It was so dark, I decided to leave, until I remembered my new flashlight. I pulled it out and twisted the end to turn it on. Even though it was small, the light was powerful. I shone it slowly around until it caught MacDuff's yellow eyes. He was crouched on his belly, staring me down the way he does when he wants to keep a sheep from moving. "What's wrong?" I asked. My voice was kind of squeaky and a little shiver went up my back.

"There's nothing to be afraid of," I whispered, shining the light up into the branches. "It's a perfect hideout," I told myself, thinking if my friend Jimmy were here, we'd make it into a fort and call it our grapevine house.

MacDuff was exploring the shadows, and I followed him with my light. Suddenly he growled, and that's when I saw the blankets. They were folded up neatly on a big pile of spruce boughs, as if someone had made a bed there. The light wobbled in my hand, but I made myself tiptoe closer. An old green backpack lay open on the ground, next to a cooking pot holding a mug, a tin plate, and a jar of matches. Two big silver cans with wire handles dangled from a branch nearby, and on top of the blankets was something that really spooked me: a half-eaten candy bar, with the wrapper torn open.

I froze, and then I was running, bumping my head as I stumbled out of the shelter. Branches whipped my face and caught at my clothes, but I never stopped until I reached the field. I ran all the way back to the cabin, looking behind me every few feet. No one was there but MacDuff, panting at my heels as if I were a sheep and he were bringing me home.

The cabin was empty. "Grandfather!" I yelled. I ran over the hill and down to the sheep pens. He was fixing a low spot in the fence, tightening the wire with his fencing tool.

"Grandfather!" I called again. He straightened up and squinted at me.

"What's wrong—you seen the ghost?"

"Don't tease," I gasped. "Someone's living out here." I told him what I'd found.

He frowned. "Probably left from last summer,"

he said. "Teenagers come out and use the island.
They want to get away from home, and I can't say as
I blame them. Used to do the same thing myself."

"You did?" I caught my breath and stared. I
couldn't imagine Grandfather running away from
his farm. "Where did you go?"

"Rice Hill. Built a little place up there with a
friend. We called it our 'cabin,' but it wasn't much
more than a crude lean-to." He grinned. "We used
to steal Pa's tobacco and roll our own cigarettes.
Thought we were pretty daring."

I laughed. "Was your pa mad?"

"Don't think he ever noticed. Anyway, I bet
that's what you found here—someplace where kids
can escape. No harm in it, long as they don't disturb
the sheep. Maybe they're the ones who took my
rope." He picked up an old bucket. "Tide's out.
Let's go down to the beach and gather some food for
dinner."

I followed him to a rocky cove, thinking hard.
Teenagers wouldn't fold their blankets so neatly,
not if they were like Ginny. You practically needed
a stick of dynamite to get into *her* room lately. And
who would leave *half* a candy bar? *I* sure wouldn't.
Unless . . . someone heard me coming and went
away in a hurry.

I didn't like that idea one bit. I caught up with
Grandfather, who was walking with his head down,

checking the rocks for mussels. "Grandfather, how long does someone's scent stay around—I mean, so MacDuff could smell it?"

"Depends," Grandfather said. "Out here, with all the rain we've had, not too long."

I shivered. "MacDuff acted like someone was in the shelter. He was growling—"

"Now, Gabriel." Grandfather bent over a tide pool with the waves swishing around his boots. He tugged at a mussel, dropped it in the pail, and smiled from under his bushy eyebrows. "He might have smelled a coon or a porcupine. Don't let your imagination run wild. Concentrate on our dinner instead."

"I'm not imagining things." I bit my lip. I could feel my face getting red, and my eyes were smarting. "Anyway, I don't like mussels."

"Good," Grandfather said, laughing, "more for me." He patted me as if I were about four years old. "Get those worries out of your curly head. I brought hot dogs, too."

I followed him along the shore, scuffing my feet and looking behind me every few steps. The beach was empty, and there was nothing in the grass beside us but an old ewe nibbling at the seaweed, her tiny hooves slipping on the smooth stones.

3

The Song in the Grass

As the sun slowly went down, Grandfather and I collected a bucketful of shiny, fat mussels, plucking them from the wet rocks in the tidepools. "Don't take any open ones," Grandfather reminded me. "They're dead." After we had a dozen or more, Grandfather dumped the mussels on a flat rock and let me clean them. I scraped off the barnacles with my jackknife, cutting away the hairy "beards" that poked through the tightly closed shells. When I nicked my finger, I sucked it quickly, to get rid of the blood before Grandfather noticed. Then we lowered the scrubbed shells into a bucket of clean seawater. "Good job," Grandfather said.

I felt warm inside. Maybe I was only clumsy when Ginny was around.

I went wading and found an oyster under a rock.

Grandfather was excited when I brought him the big, knobby shell. "A Belor oyster—you have sharp eyes!" He pried it open with his knife and showed me the soft, slippery creature inside. "Want a taste?" he asked.

I made a face. "Not while it's still alive."

Grandfather smiled. "Best not to think about it." He scraped the oyster loose from its watery bed, opened his mouth and swallowed it in one bite, then wiped his mouth with his shirtsleeve.

"Delicious!" he said.

"Yuk." I stuck out my tongue.

We built a fire on the beach and roasted hot dogs and mussels on a rusty grill. For a little while, I forgot about the shelter in the woods. The meat spattered and popped, its smell mixing with the driftwood smoke. When the mussels opened, Grandfather took them off the grill, squeezed a little lemon on each one, then scooped out the meat with his fingers. "Saves dishes." He handed me two hot dog rolls and grinned. "Here's *your* plate."

We shared an orange and an apple and then Grandfather pulled a candy bar from his jacket pocket. "Energy," he said, giving me half. The first bite was sweet, but then I remembered the open candy bar in the shelter. I edged closer to Grand-father, wishing the sun wouldn't go down so fast.

After supper, the wind came up and the tide

crept toward our campfire. "Time to go in," Grandfather said. We filled the old wheelbarrow with
driftwood and brought it to the cabin. Grandfather
built a fire in the stove, put some water on to boil,
and looked at my face. "You could use a wash. We'll
get some more water from the well."

I followed him outside. It was almost dark. When
I unzipped my jacket pocket, looking for my flashlight, the pocket was empty. I checked my pants,
then my sweatshirt. No luck. I must have dropped
it in the grapevine shelter. What would I say to
Uncle Paul? I'd always wanted a light like that, and
now I'd lost it on the first day. I could almost hear
Ginny saying, "Boy, are you stupid." And what
about tonight, when I had to sleep in the dark?

I ran to catch up with Grandfather. He was
shining his big flashlight through the tall grass near
the well. "That's funny," he said, pushing his cap
back from his forehead.

"What?"

"I could have sworn I left the bucket right here,
last time I was out." He tapped the wooden well
cover.

We searched around the bushes until I stubbed
my toe on something hard. "Here it is!" I called,
pulling out a metal bucket with a long rope attached.

Grandfather studied the way the rope was tied to
the handle. "Strange—I always use a bowline, not a

half hitch," he muttered to himself as he slid the heavy wooden cover to the side and lowered the bucket into the dark hole. We waited a long time for the splash.

"How deep is it?" I asked.

"Twenty or thirty feet," he said. "I'm glad I didn't have to dig it. It's been here since the island was first farmed."

We hauled the bucket back up together, and Grandfather pulled a rag from his pocket. "Here's your facecloth," he said. We took turns washing our face and hands in the cold water. It smelled like the mud flats at low tide. "Not fit to drink unless it's boiled," Grandfather said.

"If someone lived in that grapevine house, how would they get fresh water?" I asked.

Grandfather looked down at me. His long arms hung by his sides. "Are you still on that idea?" he said. "No one lives out here, Gabe. It's too harsh. And what would they eat?"

"Mussels and oysters—like you did tonight. Besides," I insisted, "someone used your bucket, didn't they?"

He shrugged. "Maybe. Tell you what. When the shearing's done tomorrow, you take me to that place you found, and we'll have a look."

For a minute, I felt relieved. I could get my flashlight back and Uncle Paul would never know

I'd lost it. I followed Grandfather to the cabin, trying to match my footsteps to his long strides. Suddenly, I heard a sharp, bleating sound and then a low crooning noise. I stood still. It sounded like a woman singing a sad song, like the tunes my mom hums under her breath when she's braiding Ginny's hair.

"Grandfather!" I called. "Listen!"

He cocked his head, then twisted a finger around inside his ear. "Can't always hear as good as I'd like," he complained. "What was it?"

"It sounded like a lamb bleating, and someone singing. I swear."

He frowned. "Too early for lambs, I hope—but I could be wrong. We'll see when we round up the sheep tomorrow."

"But I heard a woman crying, or something."

He touched my shoulder. "It was probably a gull. Laughing gulls sound that way."

"I know what a laughing gull sounds like. This was different."

"Some other animal, then," Grandfather said.

"Do you think it's a ghost?"

He laughed. "Afraid not, Gabriel. Must be Winny, my lead sheep. Her bleating always reminds me of an old woman."

I'd never heard a sheep sound like *that*, but Grandfather had already started back to the cabin. I hurried to keep up. The gnarled tree beside the path looked like a witch, and when I heard galloping footsteps, I whirled. Two sheep spooked behind me and took off through the tall grass. I ran so close to Grandfather's heels that I bumped into him when he stopped.

He looked down at me. "A little scared?"

"Uh-uh." I shook my head no, but I was. "Are there any lights in the cabin?" I asked. Maybe Ginny was wrong.

"Sure," he said, opening the door. "There's old-fashioned light, the best kind." Grandfather struck a match, lit a kerosene lamp, and set it on the table. The light made a warm circle, away from the shadows, and the cabin seemed cozy and safe. "Hot chocolate?" Grandfather asked.

"Great," I said. I curled up on an old sheepskin and scratched MacDuff's belly.

When Grandfather gave me a tin mug full of hot chocolate, I sat at the table, blowing on the steam to cool the cocoa while the wind whistled softly outside, making little hissing sounds in the stove. I was so cozy, I hoped Grandfather had forgotten about the ghost, but he pulled his chair up beside me and said: "That old island wind makes me think it's time for a story."

He took off his faded blue cap, took a sip from his mug, and began.

4

The Dairymaid

Sixty years ago, Grandfather told me, a family farmed on the island. "They kept cows, a pig, sheep, some chickens. Cut their hay with horses. Raised all their own food."

"Were you alive then?" I asked.

"Why sure," Grandfather answered. "I was about your age."

I leaned my elbows on the table. I love the way Grandfather tells a story. His voice is raspy and dry, like sandpaper rubbing over a rock, and he always stops at the good parts to give it suspense.

"Their house was just down the hill here, on the way to the pens. You can still see the old foundation. And the family had lots of kids, but the children were lonesome on the island. As soon as they were grown up, they moved away.

"All but the youngest," Grandfather said. "She stayed with her folks. Grew to be a pretty girl. Very small and dainty, they say; wore a long brown braid wrapped around her head like a crown."

The stove made a ticking noise. Something sighed outside but Grandfather didn't seem to notice. He was staring into the smoky chimney of the lamp. Could he see the old people inside the flame? I inched my chair a little closer to his.

"Her job was to take the milk to the dairy on the mainland," Grandfather said. "Know where Barnes's Fish Market is now, on the edge of town?" I nodded. "That was a dairy, back then. They made butter and cheese."

"How did she bring the milk over?" I asked.

"Depended on the tides. If it was high water, she rowed. At dead low, she could walk the break-water—people said she was light-footed and agile as a gymnast. She always carried two old-fashioned milk cans—tall ones, with lids and long wire handles."

I felt cold all over, even though the hot stove was right behind me. Milk cans. That's what I'd seen in the grapevine house. I opened my mouth to tell him, but Grandfather kept right on talking. Suddenly I wished he would take me on his lap, the way he did when I was little.

"She fell in love with a man at the dairy. They

were courting and he promised they'd be wed. After she delivered the milk, they'd sit outside under a big elm tree to talk and steal some kisses."

Kisses. I made a face and Grandfather chuckled. "You'll change your tune in a few years."

I didn't believe him. Naomi Sims had kissed me on the playground at school. Her kisses were wet and sticky; she even tasted like bubble gum.

"Go on," I said.

"The young couple enjoyed each other's company. People say the dairymaid was so happy, you could hear her singing as she picked her way over the slippery stones."

I licked my lips, thinking of the sounds I'd just heard. "What did she sing?"

"Love songs and ballads, I suppose. Well, one day she stayed a little too long and the tide began to turn. Her sweetheart begged her to wait until morning, but she said her mother would worry if she didn't get home. So she picked up her empty cans and started along the breakwater."

Grandfather spread his hands out flat on the table. All their lines and creases seemed deeper in the light from the lantern. "We're getting to the scary part," he warned, his blue eyes like crinkly slits.

"Don't stop now!" I said, even though something icy rippled along my spine.

"All right. Well, she was used to the breakwater, you know. Maybe she thought she could beat the tide. Maybe she thought there'd be enough moonlight—or perhaps she planned to swim the last little way." He stopped talking. The wind hissed outside the cabin.

"What happened?" I whispered.

"She never got home," Grandfather said in a low, spooky voice. "Next morning they found the milk cans, floating near the breakwater. The girl was gone."

The stove muttered and purred behind me. MacDuff twitched in his sleep, dreaming. "She drowned," I said.

"Maybe," Grandfather said. "Unless she was a Silky."

I knew about Silkies from one of my mom's songs. They were seals that became women and then went back to the ocean after living awhile with men.

"What was her name?" I asked.

Grandfather frowned and plucked at one eyebrow, trying to remember. "Celia?" he said. "No, that's not right—Delia, that was it. Delia Simpson."

"What happened to her parents?" I asked.

"They were pretty upset," Grandfather said. "They kept to themselves, and the mother hardly ever visited the mainland after that. When the war came, they sold the farm to the Hawkins family, who own it now."

"What about the ghost?" I didn't want to know, but I had to ask him.

Grandfather's voice came out hollow and deep, like someone talking in a tunnel. "They say at night, when the tide is out and the moon is full, she still walks the breakwater, calling for her lost lover, and swinging her empty milk cans to and fro—"

He stopped. "Goodness, Gabriel, those big black eyes of yours are about to pop out of your head. It's only a story, remember?"

I was trying to forget the cans I'd seen in the grapevine house. Maybe I'd only imagined them. "Grandfather—do you believe in ghosts?"

I thought he'd say no, but he made me feel worse by answering, "Sometimes." He cleared his throat. "There are lots of creaks in my old farmhouse I can't explain. Now and then I wonder if my pa's come back to tell me how to behave."

I stuck my fingers in my ears. "That's enough!"

He laughed. "All right. No more ghosts tonight. We ought to get some sleep, anyway. We've got a big day tomorrow."

5

A Face at the Window

When we went to bed, Grandfather set his big flashlight on the floor between us. "In case you need to get up in the night," he said.

"Thanks." I snuggled into my sleeping bag, glad he'd forgotten about Uncle Paul's present. Anyway, after hearing that ghost story, there was no way I'd go outside tonight, even with Grandfather's powerful light.

I closed my eyes and pretended I was at home, telling myself I couldn't see my night-light because I was under the covers. But it was hot and stuffy inside the bag, and pretty soon I had to come up for air. The room was as black as the inside of a closet. The wind made a swooshing sound and then something scrabbled on the front porch.

"Grandfather!" I hissed, "what's that noise?"

"Sheep," he muttered, sounding sleepy and cross. "Now go to sleep, Gabe."

Go to sleep, go to sleep. Grown-ups always think that will fix everything. Don't they know bad dreams can be worse than spooky sounds?

Pretty soon, Grandfather was snoring. He sounded like Uncle Paul's lobster boat when it's idling—chug, chug, sigh. Chug, chug, sigh.

The pieces of Grandfather's story were all mixed up in my mind, like fish swimming every which way in a net. I thought about everything I'd seen and heard: the milk cans and the blankets; the weird voice singing. Maybe the dairymaid was haunting the island, trying to make us go home. Then I remembered something, and it surprised me so much I sat up in bed. The candy bar. Ghosts don't eat, do they? And the well. Someone took the coiled rope and tied it to Grandfather's bucket. Does a ghost drink water?

Even though she's a pain in the butt, I almost wished Ginny were here with me. I hate to admit it, but she's good at figuring things out. And she's not afraid of the dark. In the summer, she even sleeps out in her tent alone, for the fun of it. Crazy.

I must have gone to sleep, because the next time I opened my eyes, the wind had stopped and I could hear the ocean gently pounding the rocks. I turned over and tried to go back to sleep but I couldn't; I had to pee. If only I hadn't finished that giant mug of cocoa.

"Grandfather?" I whispered, but he didn't hear me. The moon shone through our window. At least I could see what I was doing. I bumped into Grandfather's bed, looking for my sneakers. I was hoping he'd wake up, but he kept right on snoring, his chest rising and falling under his old quilted sleeping bag.

I took the big flashlight and went out on the porch, trying not to step in sheep droppings. I hurried to the edge and peed into the tall grass. MacDuff came out behind me. As I pulled up my pajamas, he started to growl. I jumped back into the doorway.

"What is it?" I whispered. He growled again, then bounced to the edge of the porch where he stood barking with his body stiff.

"What's going on?" Grandfather came up behind me. His bony legs were the color of his old gray nightshirt.

"I don't know." I could hardly talk. My heart was doing something funny all the way up into my neck.

"Duffer, cut that out," Grandfather commanded, snapping his fingers. But MacDuff growled deep in his throat, then jumped off the porch and disappeared in the tall grass.

"MacDuff, come here now," Grandfather

snapped. He whistled between his teeth and took the flashlight from me, shining it out across the field. "MacDuff!" Grandfather commanded again. MacDuff crept back to the porch, glancing behind him as if he didn't want to come in.

We went inside. MacDuff dropped down onto the sheepskin rug near the door, but he kept growling and his ears stood up like triangles.

"What's out there?" I asked, shivering.

"Nothing, I suspect," Grandfather said, but I could tell he was wondering, too. He stood in the middle of the room, listening, before we got back in bed.

"Maybe MacDuff saw the ghost," I said.

"Some animal, most likely." Grandfather yawned. His bed creaked as he shifted onto his back.

I jumped when a hand gripped my shoulder, but it was only Grandfather, reaching across. "Take it easy," he said in a scratchy voice. "I'm sorry I told you that story. We both know there's no such thing as a ghost, don't we?"

"I guess so," I said.

In a few minutes, he was snoring again. My ears seemed to get bigger and bigger, trying to pick up tiny sounds. The moonlight shone on Grandfather's lumpy body and on the pile of clothes heaped on the rickety chair. Then a bright light flashed into my eyes. I shut them quickly, and when I opened them, something had covered the moon. I squinted at the window, and my throat was as tight as the time I choked on a peach pit. A woman's face floated across the glass, like a big fish going by in an aquarium. I rubbed my eyes, praying I was dreaming, and when I looked again, she was gone.

"Grandfather!" I cried, "someone's at the window! I swear." MacDuff barked in the other room. My heart was hammering. I clutched my sleeping bag with my hands while Grandfather sat up in bed, pulled his nightshirt over his knees, and went to the door, grumbling. I couldn't stay there alone, so I followed him out onto the porch and waited while he and MacDuff circled the cabin. The flashlight disappeared, then came bobbing back around the other side. I pressed up tight against the doorframe, holding my breath and wishing I had my own flashlight in my hand.

"No one's there," he said when he came back. "Your imagination's working too hard, Gabriel. Go back to bed."

I was all worked up. If it was just my imagination, why did MacDuff bark? Grandfather didn't seem to think about that; he just scrunched into his bag and went back to sleep.

I buried my head so I couldn't see the window. Did the ghost want us out of her house? Ghosts can go through walls, can't they? Or slip through the cracks in a door? I remembered those dumb cartoons, where a ghost oozes through a keyhole and opens like a parachute on the other side. But this wasn't a chubby white sheet with a friendly smile. This ghost had a woman's face; it could sing, eat candy bars, and shine lights in windows—

I sat up. That light in my eyes—was the ghost carrying *my* flashlight around? I couldn't stand it. "Duffer, come here now," I said softly. MacDuff's claws scuffled across the wood floor in the other room, and then I felt his cold nose in my hand. "Come on," I whispered, patting my bed, "up here." MacDuff nuzzled me, then put his paws on my stomach, whining. He knows he's supposed to sleep by the door, but I grabbed his collar and pulled until he scrambled up onto the bed beside me. He pawed at my bag, making a nest, and nearly pushed me off the bed, but I didn't care. I finally fell asleep with my arms wrapped tight around his neck and my face buried in his fur.

6

The Ghost of Lost Island

I dreamed I was out in a boat, rolling from side to side in the swells, and woke up with my bed rocking up and down. "Quit it, MacDuff," I mumbled, burying my head in my sleeping bag. I hate waking up early. The bed bounced harder and I put out my hand to push the dog away. Instead of fur, I felt someone's fingers. I threw the bag off and sat up, sputtering.

My stupid sister was sitting at the end of the bed, lifting her feet and pointing her toes as if she were in ballet class. I was so disgusted I wanted to spit.

"What are *you* doing here?"

"Uncle Paul said I could come help." Ginny snapped her gum as she talked.

I groaned. Didn't Uncle Paul know this was supposed to be my special time alone with him and

Grandfather? "Get off my bed," I said. "You're giving me a headache."

"Aw, so sorry—poor little Gabe." Ginny tried to stroke my forehead, but I batted her hand away. "Grandfather told me to wake you," she said. "We have to round up the sheep."

"So get out and I'll get dressed," I said.

"Excuse *me*," Ginny said, twitching her braid across my nose. "I guess you couldn't be nice and say hello."

"No, I couldn't," I said. Why had I wished she were here last night? I'd forgotten how fast she could ruin everything.

"Better wear your sweatshirt," she said in her bossy voice. "It's cold outside." She flounced out the door.

"Miss Know-it-all," I muttered as I got dressed. It was awful having Ginny here. I wanted to be the only one helping with the shearing. Now Grandfather and Uncle Paul would give her the best jobs. No matter how hard I tried, I always dropped things or looked stupid when my sister was around. I felt like crying, but I knew it wouldn't do any good. I was stuck with her for now. Unless I got lucky, and the ghost came to take her away.

The ghost. I'd almost forgotten about last night. I looked out the window, but everything seemed normal with the sun sparkling on the ocean and someone—it looked like Uncle Paul—working on the sheep pens halfway down the hill. Maybe it was all a bad dream.

I opened the door and went to the table. Ginny puckered her lips, crossed her eyes, and blew an enormous pink bubble that stuck to her face. I ignored her and sat down in front of a steaming bowl of oatmeal.

"Eat up," Grandfather said. "Sixty ewes to shear—we'll have a busy day."

I sprinkled lots of brown sugar in the bowl and picked at my cereal. I'm never hungry in the morning.

"So," Ginny asked, blowing another bubble, "see the ghost last night?"

I stared. How did she know already? Before I could answer, she added, "Didn't Grandfather tell you that story? About the ghost who walks the breakwater?"

"Oh, *that*," I said as if I didn't care, looping my spoon through the oatmeal.

"Bet it scared you." She glanced at Grandfather. He was bent over his knapsack, with his red suspenders dangling from his waist.

"Why should it?" I answered quietly. "It's only a story."

"Maybe," she said. "Or maybe there *is* a ghost. A ghost who will come to get you, in the dark of the night, when the werewolves howl . . ." She hovered over me like some ugly bird about to pounce.

"Get out of here," I said, pushing her away. I tried to eat my oatmeal as if nothing was wrong. If she knew how freaked I'd been last night, she'd be teasing me all day. I hoped Grandfather wouldn't say anything.

Uncle Paul pushed the screen door open. His eyes were bright and his straight, sandy hair looked greased. I couldn't help smiling at him, even if he had brought Ginny along.

"Nippy out there!" he said, rubbing his hands. "Got any coffee, Pop?" While Grandfather poured him a cup, he clapped me on the shoulder. "Hope you don't mind your sister being here," he said. "Lenny was supposed to come with me, but he twisted his ankle."

"That's okay," I said, but only because I like Uncle Paul. He and his wife Annie don't have any kids. When Ginny and I go over, they don't care if we eat cookies right before dinner, and they know it's more fun to sit on their porch roof, watching the tuna boats come into Stone Harbor, than to go to bed on time.

"Your new light come in handy last night?" Uncle Paul asked.

I almost choked on my cereal. Uncle Paul clapped me on the shoulder. "Sorry—I shouldn't ask you questions when your mouth's full." He went back outside, slurping his coffee. I hoped he hadn't noticed my red face.

Grandfather sat down to lace his heavy boots. "First thing to do is drive the sheep in," he said. "We'll sweep the island starting at the north end." He squinted at me. "Finish up, Gabe."

"I'm done." I pushed my bowl away.

Grandfather took a toothpick from his jackknife and cleaned his teeth while he talked. "All right, Gabriel and Virginia, put on your boots. No dawdling or squabbling."

Ginny and I glanced at each other. It sounded as if Grandfather meant business. We pulled on our tall rubber boots and went outside. MacDuff was jumping and circling, herding imaginary sheep.

We started across the meadow. Sheep were grazing all over the field, but they bunched together when they saw us coming and took off toward the woods. "Spread out!" Grandfather called. I ran to the right, staying as far away from Ginny as I could. I was glad I had my boots on. The wet grass soaked my jeans up above my knees.

When we reached the end of the field, the sheep spooked and split apart into little groups. A couple of ewes headed for the bluff where I'd found the grapevine house. I did *not* want to go up there again, but Grandfather yelled, "Gabriel, see if you

can head them off!" I started to protest, but he and
Uncle Paul were already too far away to hear me,
and Ginny was headed in the opposite direction,
waving her arms at a black ewe to shoo it along. I
scrambled up the hill, trying to make it look as if I
were hurrying. I'd already decided there was no
way I'd go back to the shelter alone. Not after what
I'd seen last night. When the sheep bolted into the
woods, I ducked behind a big spruce tree at the
edge of the bluff so everyone would think I'd gone
after them. I peeked around the trunk to make sure
I was hidden from Ginny. The sheep went on
without me; I heard the soft thump of their hooves
on the pine needles and then it was quiet. MacDuff
will find them later, I told myself. That's his job.

Grandfather and Uncle Paul were working the
dog now; I could hear Grandfather calling, "Come
by, come by!" in the distance. Down in the field,
the white tip of MacDuff's tail bobbed as he circled
to the left around a big clump of sheep. They bolted
and Grandfather shouted, "Way to me!" His voice
faded away as he and Uncle Paul jogged across the
field. I waited until I could see Ginny running
behind them, tripping in the tall grass. I was about
to come out from behind the tree when I heard a
twig snap. Had the sheep come back?

I peered out, but there was no sign of the ewes.
The twisting, shadowy path disappeared into the

moss-covered trees. The sheep had probably run right past the grapevine house. Was the ghost hiding there? Would the sheep see her, or was she only visible to humans? I thought about a book I'd read once, where the kids in the story could see a ghost but the grown-ups couldn't, so they thought the kids were lying. Maybe that's what was happening to me.

My mouth was all dry. Stop it, I told myself. Don't think about the ghost now. But I couldn't help it. If only I were brave enough to follow the sheep, to crawl into the shelter, find my flashlight, and see if anyone had been there since yesterday. But I wasn't, and I never would be. Grandfather would be mad at me for letting the sheep go; Ginny would criticize me. Too bad, I thought, watching her run across the field behind the black ewe, flapping her arms like a bird. "Go on," I whispered, bouncing nervously from one foot to the other, "hurry up, so I can come out."

"Who's there?"

I whirled around. A sharp, rusty voice seemed to come from right beside me and from far away at the same time, scraping through me like someone drawing long, sharp fingernails down a chalkboard. I couldn't see anyone. My heart hammered against my ribs. I wanted to run, but it was like one of those bad dreams where a monster chases you and your legs are rooted to the ground. I stood there, frozen, while a phantom shape drifted smoothly through the dark woods. The thing seemed to have no color; maybe it was only a shadow, or maybe the trees, with their dangling, gray-green moss, were playing tricks on me, but it sure looked like a ghost. There was a flutter of cloth, a short, pitiful cry, and then something bright flashed in a patch of sunlight. My legs came unstuck, and without looking where I was going, I was running faster than I knew how, away from the haunted woods toward the ocean.

7

"Gone, But Not Forgotten"

I ran with my arms and legs pumping, down the hill and across the meadow, until I heard Uncle Paul's voice boom out. When I stopped to catch my breath, I was on a rocky cliff above the secret cove. A bunch of sheep ran past, their feet clicking on the stones. MacDuff was right behind them, crisscrossing at their heels. I clambered over the rocks onto the beach just as Grandfather ran by, huffing and puffing, his long arms swinging from side to side.

Uncle Paul beckoned to me, and I hurried to keep up. "Did you lose those sheep?" he called over his shoulder.

"I didn't mean to!" I cried. "Uncle Paul, wait—"

"Don't worry!" he yelled, dashing after two ewes that had broken from the flock.

"Way to me!" Grandfather shouted.

MacDuff darted to the right, circled around the two sheep, and brought them back.

"Gabe, you stay behind," Uncle Paul called. "Drive them forward. With the water on one side and the cliffs on the other, they can't get away." He and Grandfather ran beside the sheep, flailing their arms and hooting to keep the ewes bunched up together. MacDuff and I trotted behind.

It was low tide, and the rocks were slippery. Every time I thought of what I'd seen, my palms felt sweaty and my neck prickled. Was it all in my imagination? Not the voice. I knew I'd heard a voice. But who was it? Maybe Grandfather was right. Maybe some teenagers were hiding out here, and they'd tried to scare me so I wouldn't give them away. Well, they didn't have to worry. I wouldn't go near those woods again.

Around the next point, the field came right down to the ocean. I chased a ewe when she veered into the tall grass. Suddenly she screeched to a halt, then started running around, frantic, in circles. She was trapped inside a low, iron fence. I followed her, squeezing through a broken gate, before I realized we were caught in a tiny graveyard. A few lonely, gray headstones leaned toward the ocean. The ewe seemed as spooked as I was; she gathered her legs and jumped the fence, heading straight back to the flock.

Before I could follow her, I tripped on a broken headstone and fell flat in the long grass.

"Oof. That hurt." I propped myself up on my elbows and stared. Right in front of me was a crooked gravestone streaked with dirty black lines. All the other stones in the cemetery were surrounded by tall grass and weeds, but this one was different. Someone had clipped away the grass and brush, leaving a smooth place in front. A tiny bouquet of violets in an old soda bottle leaned against the gravestone. Even though it was sunny, the violets were hardly wilted, as though they'd just been set there.

"Oh, man, this is really getting weird." I got to my feet slowly, thinking of all the dead people lying under my feet, and made myself look at the headstone. A carved, chubby angel with spreading wings looked down on the words: DELIA LEMARE SIMPSON, and below the name, in dark chiseled letters, it said, GONE, BUT NOT FORGOTTEN.

Delia Simpson. Wasn't that the ghost's name? But how could she be buried here, if they never found her body? The violets on her grave were the creepiest part of all. I dashed back to the shore without looking to see if anything was following me.

When I caught up to the flock, the sheep were moving fast. "Way round!" Grandfather bellowed. MacDuff streaked past us, the white brush on his tail flickering in the tall grass.

"Git down!" Grandfather commanded.

MacDuff whirled and faced the sheep in a crouch, his belly just above the ground, his yellow eyes staring the sheep down. The whole flock tumbled together, bobbing like a giant woolly blanket. Then Grandfather sent MacDuff to the back and the sheep started forward again.

We ran them beside the field. I was really happy when I saw the cabin up to the right and then the long section of fence Grandfather and I had set up. My lungs were aching, and I *had* to talk to Grandfather, but he couldn't pay attention to me yet. "Come by, come by," Grandfather yelled. MacDuff herded most of the sheep toward the pen, except for three ewes that bolted up the hill. The sheep pushed and shoved, trying to escape as we funneled them into our chute.

"Gabe!" Grandfather shouted, "give us a hand!" I helped him move the sides of the chute closer together while Uncle Paul braced one of our movable panels across the open end of the V. When the flock was trapped inside, Grandfather whistled to MacDuff, who jumped the fence, ran across the backs of all the sheep, and dropped to the ground behind them.

"MacDuff, git down!" Grandfather ordered.

MacDuff crouched, panting, and the sheep stood still, bunched into a circle.

I pulled off my sweatshirt and flopped on the ground, gasping for breath, while MacDuff and Grandfather slowly maneuvered the sheep from the chute into the holding pen. Grandfather took out a handkerchief and wiped his face. Sweat was trickling down his neck.

"Pop, you're running yourself ragged." Uncle Paul's voice was hoarse and deep, like some of the old ewes. "Why don't you rest? Gabe and I can round up the next bunch."

"Don't be silly," Grandfather said. "MacDuff's used to working with me. Anyway, even though I'm huffing and puffing, I'm still having a good time." He started up the hill. "Got to catch the three that got away," he said.

"Grandfather—" I began, but he said, "Gabe, you can help most by staying here. Count them, and keep a close watch to make sure they don't bash the fence down."

"Do I have to stay here alone?" I gulped.

He frowned. "Come on, Gabe, it's broad daylight. What are you worried about *now*?"

I hesitated. Grandfather didn't usually sound so gruff; I guess he was just in a hurry. "Nothing," I said. "It's just—well, I found a gravestone that said 'Delia Simpson' and it spooked me. Isn't that the ghost's name?"

Uncle Paul gave me a soft punch on the arm.

"Did Pop scare you with that story last night? Shame on you," he said, wagging his finger at Grandfather. "Don't worry, Gabriel," he said, "ghosts don't come out in the daytime. You only have to worry about them in the dead of night. Right, Pop?"

I wanted Grandfather to say there was no such thing as a ghost, day or night, but he was checking his watch. "Ginny will be along shortly. We have at least eight or nine sheep missing—it will help if you give us an exact count when we come back. Thanks, Gabe."

It was hard to argue with Grandfather, so I just watched as he and Uncle Paul went up the hill. The face at the window, the moving shadow in the trees, and the old gravestone all pointed to one thing as far as I was concerned: the ghost was haunting the island, even in broad daylight. Maybe she wanted us to leave.

For a minute, I even wished my sister would show up. At least I wouldn't be alone. But there was no sign of her, so I made myself count the ewes. It's easy in cartoons, where sheep jump over a wall one at a time. In real life, they're all bunched together and you can lose track easily. The first time, I got forty-nine, then fifty. Finally, I got fifty-one twice, and decided that was close enough.

When the sheep settled down a little, I walked up

the hill until I could see the ocean. Whitecaps were churning toward the mainland, and waves smashed against the base of the breakwater, sending spray up over the rocks even though the tide was still pretty low.

Oh, no. Was I seeing things again? I shielded my eyes with my hand. Something was moving out there. "It's not the ghost; please, say it isn't," I breathed, but the ghost—or something—was out on the breakwater, halfway between the island and the mainland. The sun was glaring into my eyes, making it hard to see, and the figure was so far away, I thought it might be a signal buoy, rocking in the waves, or a stranded porpoise. But it definitely had a woman's shape, with long, fluttering skirts. I backed slowly up the hill to get a better view, keeping my eyes glued to the small figure. Something bright blinked in the sunshine, swinging next to the colorless shape as it crept along the rocks.

I watched until it reached the pile of rocks called Murphy's Lookout; after that, I couldn't see it anymore. Even though the sun was still warm, I shivered and rubbed my hands up and down my arms, taking another step backward.

"Gabe, watch out!" Ginny's voice was right under my feet. I whirled around. My sister was standing in a big square hole behind me with her elbows resting on a stone wall.

"Man, you really surprised me," I complained, although I was almost getting used to it. They should call this place "The Island of Surprises."

"I was afraid you might fall in," Ginny said. "What are you doing?"

I cleared my throat. Ginny would only laugh if I told her what I'd seen. "Uh—nothing much. Just watching the sheep for Grandfather. What *is* this place?"

"It looks like a cellar hole."

The old foundation. Of course. Grandfather said the dairymaid's house was on this hillside. I crouched on the edge and looked in. Four sturdy stone walls held up the sides. A small birch tree grew out of the middle, where the dirt floor would have been, and at the far end was a crumbling chimney. It looked safer than any other place I'd been all day. I hate to admit it, but I was actually glad to see my sister.

"The people who farmed the island must have lived here," Ginny said when I jumped into the hole. "Look." She pointed to an iron washtub. "How'd you like to take a bath in that?" Then she showed me a huge iron pot with a handle, the kind I always imagine a witch would use. "Here's their cooking pot—and how about this!" She picked up a pale blue bottle, crusted with dirt. "I dug it out from under the tub. It must be really old." Her eyes were glittering. "It's so lonely and sad, thinking of the people who lived here—and now they're all dead." She stared at me a minute. "Geez, Gabe, you look as if you'd seen the ghost."

"What ghost?" It seemed as if I couldn't get away from the dairymaid for more than five minutes.

"You know, Grandfather's ghost. The one in the story." She dusted off her jeans.

"Why do you keep bringing that up?" I asked, watching her face.

Ginny put her hands over her heart and closed her eyes. "It's so romantic to think the dairymaid might still be here, singing for her lost love."

Romantic? She would think of it that way. Suddenly we heard ewes blatting down at the pens.

She climbed out and stood up on tiptoe, squinting. She's supposed to wear glasses, but ever since she turned thirteen, she says they get in her way. "More sheep just came in," she said. "They're running beside the pens. We'd better go down." She beckoned to me. "We can come back and explore this later, okay?"

"Maybe." I glanced at her. Why was she being so nice to me all of a sudden?

"Come on," Ginny said.

"Hold on." I bent over near the chimney stones, pretending to tie my shoe. I wanted to check something out. When Ginny ran off without waiting for me, I stood up, pulling on a heavy rock at the base of the chimney. There was a concrete slab under the stones, and it looked as if something was carved into it; a couple of letters—*R*, maybe? And *E*? A big rock gave way; its mortar was crumbling and old, and it was sticky with moss and dirt. I shoved and pushed, throwing five or six big stones onto the ground.

Kids had carved their names around the base of the chimney, the way Ginny and I did when our dad put a new cement floor in our garage. Four names were easy to read: *Julia, Tom, Peter, Jane.* Peeking out from under a huge, flat stone were three more letters, tipped on their sides as if the person making them were just learning how to write: *D-E-L*, with the *D* written backward. I didn't have to move the stone to know what the last letters would be. Delia had been here, too.

I was out of there in an instant. As far as I could see, Delia was everyplace on this island. I ran down the hill. Three more ewes had shown up, and Ginny had forced them into the chute. The flock in the pen was baaing and bleating like a school band playing all the wrong notes while Ginny stood with her feet planted and her arms stretched wide, guarding the ones she'd captured.

"Come by, come by!" Uncle Paul and Grandfather came up over the dunes with MacDuff, who was driving the last of the sheep toward the pens. I ran to help, but by the time I got there, Ginny and Uncle Paul had herded the stragglers into the chute. I counted the extras quickly before they were in the corral.

"Fifty-nine sheep all together," I said.

Grandfather clamped a hand on Ginny's shoulder. "Did you catch these strays by yourself?"

"Yup." She tossed her braid and grinned. You'd think she'd just won the state basketball championship. Too bad her braces gleam so much when she smiles.

"Nice work. It's a good thing Paul decided to bring you today." Grandfather smiled at her, then gave me a stern look. "Gabriel, there's no harm done, but I asked you to stick with the flock. What were you doing?"

The three of them looked at me, waiting for an answer. What could I say? No one would believe I'd seen a ghost on the breakwater, and then found her name in the basement. My face felt hot and swollen. "I was exploring the old cellar hole," I said, making a circle in the grass with the toe of one boot.

"Never mind," Grandfather said at last. "Sounds as if we've got all the sheep together—although we should have sixty. You're sure it's fifty-nine?"

"Pretty sure," I said.

"We'll count them again as we work," said Grand-father. He pushed up his sleeves. "Let's get a drink from our big jug. And then, it's time for the shearing to begin."

8

The Shearing

I didn't have a second to think about the ghost after that. When we got the sheep in the pen, Grandfather gave MacDuff some dog biscuits and fresh water. Then we went to Uncle Paul's lobster boat, hoisted the generator onto a two-wheeled cart, and hauled it up the trail to the pens. It was really heavy. Grandfather and Uncle Paul swore a lot, even though Ginny and I were there.

The generator made a terrible racket and belched out a gasoline smell. "Beats shearing by hand, though," Uncle Paul said as he hitched up the electric clippers.

We went back to the boat for burlap bags and two big pieces of plywood. We put one on the ground for the sheep and set the other on two sawhorses like a table. Grandfather cleaned the plywood with a rag. "Ginny, you can skirt the fleeces," he said. "That will be a good job for your quick fingers."

I glared at my sister. Removing the dirty wool and then picking twigs and long grass from the fleece was what *I* would have done if she hadn't shown up. I was going to complain but Grandfather surprised me. "Don't look so glum, Gabriel," he said, "you're just the right size for the wool tower."

"Gabe's too small!" Ginny protested, sounding jealous.

Grandfather patted her shoulder. "Today was meant to be Gabriel's special time to help us. His strong legs will mash the fleeces down nicely."

I beamed. Grandfather had never called me strong before, and I was excited to go into a wool tower for the first time. It's a huge wooden frame, like the bottom of a giant's chair. A long burlap bag dangles from the top. When it fills up with fleeces, you climb into the bag to stomp them down. Ginny told me about it after last year's shearing.

Grandfather and Uncle Paul brought the wool tower up from the boat. It was tall; even Uncle Paul had to stand on a milk crate to hook the wool bag in place. The sack was longer than Grandfather's sleeping bag. "How will I get in there?" I asked.

"We'll hoist you," Uncle Paul said, "but let's wait until we have a stack of fleeces ready." He pointed to the bottom of the sack where someone had written

WHITE in big letters. "Don't put colored fleeces in here," he said. "The blacks and grays go in a separate bag." He ruffled my hair. "Some of these ewes have wool as dark and curly as your mop."

Grandfather and Uncle Paul stripped to the waist and put on sheepskin vests. "Ready to roll!" Uncle Paul cried, wrestling a ewe from the corral into the tiny shearing pen. He sat her on the plywood with her head lolling to the side.

Grandfather carefully oiled the clippers, let them buzz for a minute, and the shearing began.

First Grandfather clipped off the belly wool and the tags—that's what they call the dirty wool from the ewe's neck and hind end—and tossed them to the side. Then he started the real shearing, pushing the electric clippers through the thick fleece as if he were peeling a giant, woolly banana skin away from the ewe's body. The inside of the fleece was as white as cotton balls. Grandfather did the neck first, then buzzed the clippers along her shoulders, back, and sides.

When he was finished, the sheep sat small and naked in her nest of wool. Uncle Paul lifted the fleece carefully and gave it to Ginny.

While Grandfather started on the next ewe, Uncle Paul showed me how to bundle the fleece. "Roll it with the clean side out, then toss it in the wool bag."

Uncle Paul and Grandfather took turns shearing.
After we had a bunch of fleeces tied and bundled,
Uncle Paul said, "Off with those shoes, Gabriel. It's
time to dive in." I left my sneakers on the ground
and Uncle Paul hoisted me to the top of the frame.
I sat with my feet dangling for a second, then
tumbled into the sticky fleeces. I could hear Ginny
laughing outside the bag, but I was too busy flailing
around to care. The burlap was scratchy and smelly.
I held my breath; I was afraid if I opened my mouth,
I'd choke on wool. I felt as if I were swimming in a
tangle of yarn. Finally I stood up. "Stomp as hard as
you can!" Uncle Paul yelled. I remembered Grandfather saying I had strong legs, so I jumped and ran
in place, jamming my feet onto the fleeces until
they were packed tight.

"Another one coming!" Grandfather shouted. I
covered my eyes and held my breath as the fleece
skittered down my back. This was fun. There was no
way to mess things up inside the bag. When Ginny
tried to poke me from the outside, I just laughed
and pressed my nose against the burlap, making an
ugly face that she couldn't see, then flopped down
in the soft wool. I looked straight up at the sky.
Maybe this was what a rabbit saw from the bottom
of his hole.

"Want to come out?" Uncle Paul sounded far
away.

"Not yet—I'll wait for more fleeces." I curled up. The clippers buzzed, the sun warmed the bag, and I dozed. Every few minutes, another fleece tumbled into the sack and I jumped to my feet to trample it down.

The pile got higher and higher all morning, until finally I pulled myself to the top of the tower. The lanolin from the fleeces made my hands sticky, and so much wool was glued onto my socks, they looked like sheepskin slippers.

"Hey, Ginny, you can see everything from up here." Luckily, the tower was too rickety for both of us; it was nice to look down on her for a change. I took a deep breath. The damp sea air smelled clean, but every part of me stank of sheep.

Grandfather arched his back and stretched. "Whew—these old muscles need a rest," he said.

Uncle Paul rubbed his belly. "And *this* muscle needs food. How about some lunch?"

Grandfather took a quick count of the ewes that were left to shear. "Drat," he said. He took off his cap and scratched his head. From where I sat, his hair looked thin on top. "Twenty-four to go—you're sure we've shorn thirty-five?"

"Positive," Uncle Paul said.

"I guess you were right, Gabriel," Grandfather said. "There are fifty-nine here—so one old girl's still out there, playing the fox."

Uncle Paul helped me down and I looked at Grandfather. "Could any of the sheep have babies yet?"

"I don't think so." Grandfather gave me a sharp look. "Why?"

"Remember last night, I told you about that crying noise that sounded like a lamb?"

"And I couldn't hear it." Grandfather twisted a finger around in his ear and glanced at Uncle Paul, looking embarrassed. "I know, I know—'Pop, why won't you get a hearing aid?'—I'm just too stubborn, I guess." He smiled at me. "Were you thinking a missing ewe might be hiding somewhere with her baby?"

I nodded. "I think it's too early," Grandfather said, "but we'll check it out this afternoon. MacDuff can help us." He frowned. "Say, where *is* that dog?" He stuck his fingers between his teeth and let out a shrill whistle. We all waited for MacDuff to come running. Grandfather whistled again, and a gull screamed at him from overhead.

Uncle Paul laughed. "The sea gull likes you, Pop."

Grandfather rubbed his face. "Foolish dog. You suppose he's gone after the missing ewe on his own?"

I turned away. I had worse ideas about what MacDuff might be doing. If he'd seen the ghost, she might have put a spell on him—or worse. I thought about the way MacDuff had comforted me last night when I was afraid; how he always licked my face and wagged his tail when he hadn't seen me for a little while. Even though he's Grandfather's dog, he always treats me like his special friend.

"Would MacDuff cross the breakwater?" I asked.

Grandfather shook his head. "Not even if I ordered him to. He'd be scared to death—you know what he thinks about the ocean. He'll be back, I'm sure."

"Yeah, Gabe," Ginny said in her bossy voice, "don't be such a worrywart. You always think the worst things will happen."

Grandfather pulled on his old jacket. "Virginia, why don't you come help me make up some sandwiches? Give your brother a little peace."

I smirked at her and she stuck out her tongue before running up the hill.

Uncle Paul took down the wool bag and tied it closed. I helped him carry it to the open shed next to the pens. "We'll keep it here until it's time to load the boat," he said. "The weather report's calling for fog—I don't want the wool to get wet."

We walked up to the cabin together. "Don't let your sister get to you," he said, his blue eyes twinkling. "She might soften up, if you'd be a little more friendly."

I sighed. Even Uncle Paul didn't understand.

"Anyway, thirteen's not such an easy age," he was saying. "She might be easier to live with next year—but by then you'll be into it yourself."

He chuckled and I kept my head down. There was no way I'd ever be like Ginny next year. No way at all.

Uncle Paul took me by the shoulder so I had to look at him. "You know, your dad used to boss me like crazy when we were boys."

"He did?" I rubbed wisps of fleece from my eyes. Uncle Paul was so much bigger than Dad, I always forgot he was the youngest. "What did you do?"

He grinned. "I just waited a few years. One day, your dad woke up and discovered I was stronger than he was. That was the end of our fights."

I smiled at him. Imagining myself bigger than Ginny—the way I felt on top of the tower—was almost enough to push away my queasy feelings about MacDuff. Almost—but not quite.

9

Lost in the Fog

We ate our sandwiches on the porch, but Grandfather wouldn't sit down; he leaned against a post, watching the field.

"Won't you take a seat, Pop?" Uncle Paul asked, bringing a folding chair from the cabin.

"In a minute." Grandfather pulled off his cap. His thin white hair was clumped together like raked hay. "I'm just wondering where my dog's got to. It's not like Duffer to disappear." He whistled twice, and I kept watching, hoping to see the tip of MacDuff's tail flicker in the tall grass.

"Shouldn't we go look for him?" I asked, but Uncle Paul shook his head. "I'm sure he's chasing rabbits. We'll find him later. Right now we all need a rest. Especially you, Pop; come on."

Grandfather sat down, grumbling, and stretched

out his long legs. Uncle Paul leaned against the weathered boards of the cabin, turning his face up to the sun. When Ginny stepped off the porch, I grabbed her arm. "Where are you going?" I demanded.

She stared at me. "Boy, are you ever jittery. I need to use the outhouse—do you *mind*?" She twisted away, flouncing up the path. Only Ginny could make a trip to the bathroom look as if she were making an exit off a stage. I followed her a little way until I was out of sight of the cabin, then sat down under a birch tree.

"Looks as if we've had some visitors out here," Grandfather was saying to Uncle Paul in a low voice. I held still so he wouldn't know I was listening.

"Gabe told me he found blankets in a makeshift shelter," he went on. "Someone stole the rope from the flagpole; used the well and the outhouse. Even finished the roll of toilet paper!"

Uncle Paul chuckled. "Well, at least we know it's not your famous ghost. Never heard of spirits needing a bathroom."

Uncle Paul almost sounded as if he believed in the ghost, too. I clenched my hands tight so I wouldn't chew my nails.

"I haven't seen a boat, so I assume no one's around now—although MacDuff gave us quite a scare last night, barking and growling at two in the morning. I thought for sure someone was outside the cabin."

Gave *us* a scare? I didn't think Grandfather was afraid of anything. I held very still. The face was real, I thought with a shiver.

But Uncle Paul was laughing. "Sounds like you're getting carried away with your own ghost story, Pop," he said. "Must have been an animal—a bobcat, maybe? I've heard they've been seen on the islands."

"Even *I* would hear a bobcat's screech," Grandfather muttered. "And he'd leave us with a mess of injured sheep. Well, it's probably nothing to worry about—as long as MacDuff shows up."

"He will," Uncle Paul said, and then they were quiet. I peered out from behind the tree. They'd both set their caps low on their foreheads to shade their faces from the sun. A tap on my shoulder made me jump and whirl around, but it was only Ginny, crouched in the tall grass behind me. "Come here," she hissed.

I got up quietly and followed her into the field.

"Do you have to keep sneaking up on me like that?" I complained.

"Shhh!" she whispered. When we couldn't see the cabin anymore, she said, "Did you hear that? Prowlers out here on the island—who could it be?" Her cheeks were pink and her voice was all breathy and excited. "And what's this about a shelter you found?"

I hesitated. I'd promised myself that I wouldn't tell her about the grapevine house. But what good did that do, if I didn't dare go back there alone?

"Come on," Ginny prodded, "what's the big secret?"

"It's just a place in the woods where—" I caught myself. I almost said: *Where the ghost lives*. "It's— like a house made of vines, a grapevine house. There are blankets inside, and some old milk cans—"

"Milk cans!" Ginny almost shrieked. "Like the ones the dairymaid carried? Come on, Gabe, are you making that up?"

I shook my head. "Anyway, that's just a story, remember?" I said, mimicking what she'd said this morning.

She gave me this funny look. "I wonder."

Before I could ask what she meant, Grandfather called, "Gabriel! Virginia! Let's get going."

As we hurried back to the cabin, I thought about a cleaned-up gravestone, a missing rope, and children carving their names a long, long time ago. Most of all, I thought about a ghost or a prowler hurting MacDuff, which made me chew my nails right down to the quick.

The final shearing took forever, even though we had fewer sheep. Whenever it was Uncle Paul's turn with the clippers, Grandfather went off into the field to whistle for MacDuff and came back looking really discouraged. Finally, when my whole head was buzzing, they freed the last sheep and Uncle Paul shut the engine off.

I hoisted myself out of the wool bag, coughing and sputtering, and took a deep breath. A thick fog had come in; a high-pitched horn hooted from the channel, and the breakwater had disappeared. Grandfather and Uncle Paul cleaned up their tools. The air was chilly; we pulled on jackets over our sweatshirts. Then Uncle Paul tied the wool bags closed with baling twine, and Ginny and I helped him drag them to the open shed near the pens. "We'll load them in the boat tomorrow morning," Uncle Paul said.

"Aren't we going home tonight?" I asked, trying to keep my voice steady.

"Not in this weather," Uncle Paul said. "You can see why they call this 'Lost Island.' We're lost in the fog, all right. I'll radio your mom and dad. They won't mind if you stay another night."

They wouldn't mind, but I would. "What about MacDuff?" I asked, at the same time that Ginny said, "Are we going to look for that sheep?"

"That's next," Grandfather said. "I know we're all tired, but we've got to comb the island before dark.

Poor old Duffer must be in a jam somewhere—or else he's found the missing sheep and holed up with her. That's my hope."

Grandfather looked really worried. "May I come with you?" I asked him.

Grandfather frowned, his eyebrows making a white line across his forehead. "We'd cover more ground if we split up. I was hoping we could each take one section of the island. You know the lay of the land up that way, don't you?" He pointed toward the bluff where I'd found the shelter.

"Sort of." I did *not* like the way this was turning out.

Grandfather said he would walk the cliffs on the east side if Uncle Paul took the north end. "Fine," Uncle Paul said. "I want to check on the boat anyway, and radio in to shore."

"That leaves the beach and breakwater area for you, Virginia," Grandfather said. I glanced at my sister. Her face was pinched up, and she actually looked scared. Amazing. Miss Know-it-all, Miss Never Afraid of Anything—afraid? When she opened her mouth, she sounded very small.

"Couldn't Gabe and I go together?" she asked. "In case—I mean, he hasn't been here before, so he might get lost."

Grandfather smiled. "You don't need to worry

about Gabe," he said, "but if it makes you feel better, by all means stick together. Start on the beach, and then go into the woods. Just be sure you cover this side of the island." He checked his watch. "Four o'clock—let's meet back at the cabin by six or so. I don't want you out in the fog once it gets dark."

I licked my lips. *I* didn't want to be out after dark either. It would be so easy for the ghost to sneak up on us, or to follow us without our knowing it.

Ginny and I watched while Grandfather and Uncle Paul took off in opposite directions. Then I looked at my sister. Her eyes were so narrow I almost couldn't see their honey color. "You don't have to come with me, you know," I said, as if I didn't care. "Unless you're scared."

She shrugged. "There's something funny going on out here."

"Like what?"

She didn't answer. The horn out in the channel sounded like a lost owl. "Come on," I said, "let's get going."

"Hold on." Ginny cleared her throat. "Remember this morning, when I was in the cellar hole— you were looking at something on the breakwater, weren't you?"

I stared at her. "Why?"

"Promise you won't laugh."

I nodded, surprised.

"I know this sounds really strange, but I thought I saw—well, a woman walking out there. I wasn't wearing my glasses, so I couldn't tell. But then, when you got in the cellar hole, you looked freaked—as if you'd seen it, too."

"I thought I was seeing things," I admitted.

Ginny gave me a big smile, forgetting to hide her braces. "I did, too. I thought I was nuts."

Boy, things were sure changing fast. "It's almost worse, you know—that we both saw it. That means it's real—whatever it is."

Ginny pounced on me like a cat pinning down a mouse. "Do you think it's the ghost of the dairymaid? Could she be the prowler?"

"Maybe." All of a sudden, I wanted Ginny's heart to race as fast as mine was. "There was a face at my window last night," I blurted. "I heard a spooky voice in the woods this morning. And then—this is really weird—I found a little graveyard with the dairymaid's headstone. It was all cleaned up, with a bottle of flowers right beside it."

"Oooh!" Ginny hugged herself, rocking from her heels to her toes. "Gabe, do you think we'll meet a real ghost?"

"Geez, you sound like that would be the neatest thing in the world. You're really weird, you know?"

"Not really. Come on, Gabe, haven't you ever

been so scared it was delicious—like in a horror movie, or visiting a haunted house?"

I hate those things, and she knows it. "This is for real, Gin."

She shrugged. I knew she'd never admit she was scared, not in front of me. "Want to go to the grapevine house?" I asked, testing her.

"I guess." Ginny snapped her gum, but her eyes looked a little worried. "We're supposed to look for MacDuff, aren't we?"

"I think he might be up there." I told her about the bleating sound I'd heard this morning, and how a phantom, or something, was floating in the trees.

"So that's where the ghost hangs out?" Ginny asked.

"The ghost is everywhere."

Ginny looked quickly over her shoulder and we both laughed, but it was that kind of nervous giggling where you're pretending nothing's really wrong. "The thing is," I said, "if there *is* a lamb up there, MacDuff might have found it." I puffed up my chest, as if it would make me feel brave. "Ghosts are imaginary, right?"

Wrong, I thought. But Ginny said, in a fake cheerful voice, "So let's go scare ourselves to death."

We started across the field. Instead of taking the

lead, the way she usually does, Ginny stuck close to my heels. Even though my insides were quivering like a mess of Jell-O, the feeling that my sister was following *me*, made me stand up tall. Maybe I was going to grow those extra inches after all.

10

Delia

It was hard to see in front of us; long wisps of fog, like thin strands of fleece, were creeping over the field. As we hurried through the wet grass, hoping we were going in the right direction, we kept bumping into little clumps of shorn sheep. They looked like raw naked dogs, but there was no sign of the dog we really wanted. I kept glancing over my shoulder, wondering if the ghost were floating behind us.

It took us awhile to find the bluff, and when we started climbing, I wasn't sure if we were on the right trail. "There's a funny smell here," Ginny said.

I sniffed. There was a rotten stench in the air, like the time a mouse died in the wall of our house. "Let's hurry," I said. The fog made everything spooky; the big spruce tree where I'd been hiding this morning suddenly appeared in front of us.

"Listen," Ginny whispered, "what's that?"

Someone was singing in a high-pitched, quavery voice that made me feel as if little bugs were crawling inside my shirt. We dropped to the ground behind the tree, and Ginny cupped her hand over my ear. " 'Delia's Gone,' " she whispered.

I cocked my head. Sure enough, it was that depressing song our mother sings about a woman whose boyfriend shoots her on a Saturday night.

"Delia's gone, one more round, Delia's gone," the voice sang, repeating the chorus over and over. The tune was all wrong.

Ginny clutched my arm. "Listen." A high-pitched bleating sounded from the top of the hill. "It *is* a lamb," Ginny said, forgetting to whisper. "You were right."

The singing stopped suddenly; whoever it was had heard us. We huddled close together under the thick branches. I blinked; the mist was getting thick and it took me a minute to make out a woman's shape moving toward us. I jammed my fist into my mouth, trying not to cry out. At first, the woman looked like a shadow; there was no color in her long skirt with its raggedy hem, her old running shoes, or her hair, twisted into a scraggly braid on top of her head. As she came closer, we saw a pasty white face with deep grooved wrinkles. Only her eyes had color; they were a dark cold blue, like the ocean on a winter morning.

She looked a lot like the person who'd peered in my window last night. But this was an old woman, not a ghost. Or was she? Could someone older than Grandfather walk across the breakwater? Maybe this was a ghost who could make herself seem real.

"I know you're there," she said in a husky voice. "Don't play games with me."

I couldn't move. When I glanced at Ginny, she was using her fingers to pull her eyes into a squint, the way she does when she wants to see something clearly. As for me, I'd be *glad* if the woman's face were a blur—just looking at her made my breath come out fast and shallow.

Without any warning, she strode toward us and yanked the big branch aside. "*Children,*" she hissed, as if we were poisonous snakes.

We scrambled to our feet and edged away. Even though she was smaller than both of us, her face gave me the willies, and she had a sour smell, like wet wool.

We all stared at each other. My heart was pounding loud enough for everyone to hear, and Ginny was clutching my arm, digging her nails right through my sleeve.

"Who are you?" Ginny's voice was all tangled up in her throat. The old woman didn't answer. The pitiful bleating sounded up near the shelter—and then we heard a frantic yipping I recognized right away.

"MacDuff!" My voice cracked. "Come here now!"

His whines were muffled and sad; they stayed in the same place. I edged away from the old woman, praying she wouldn't grab me.

"Your dog?" The woman pointed in the direction of the shelter. "Go get him if you like. But come back—I've got something to tell you."

Ginny and I exploded from our hiding place, pushed past her, and scrambled through the trees, following MacDuff's whines. He was tied up near the shelter, with a cord knotted around his muzzle. When he saw us he leaped in the air, then flung himself against us.

"Hey, Duffer, calm down." I threw my arms around his white ruff. His body quivered all over. "Boy, are we glad to see you! We'll get you out of here in a jiffy." Ginny untied the rope while I fumbled with the knots around his nose. "Shoot," I said. "Gin, can you do this? Hurry."

She knelt beside his head. "Hold him still," she said.

I stroked him nervously, keeping an eye over my

shoulder for the old woman. "Why would she want to talk to us?"

Ginny shrugged. "How should I know? She can't hurt us—at least, I don't think so. We're bigger than she is by a long shot, and we've got MacDuff now. But she's weird, that's for sure."

In another second, MacDuff was free. "Grandfather's right," I blurted, "you do have quick fingers."

"Gee, thanks." Ginny looked surprised. MacDuff wriggled with excitement. "Where's the lamb, Duffer?" Ginny asked.

He wagged his tail, yipped, and disappeared inside the shelter, just like yesterday.

"MacDuff!" Ginny cried. "Come here!" We stuck our heads into the opening and a lamb bleated, so close that I jumped. MacDuff's rough tongue tickled my wrist.

"You've got the baby!" I cried. I patted MacDuff and peered into the gloomy shelter, wishing I had my flashlight.

"Is the mother there?" Ginny asked.

"I can't tell." I crawled in, scuttling around on the earth floor until I bumped into the lamb's shivering, damp body. I looked around quickly, but the shelter seemed empty. I scooped up the baby and backed out on my knees with Ginny right behind me. MacDuff licked our hands, his tail circling, while we stood in the clearing admiring the lamb. It was jet black, its fleece coiled tight like springs. I set it on its feet, but its tiny legs buckled.

"Come here, little one," I whispered, holding it close. Its heart beat right through my sweatshirt. Suddenly a hoarse voice shouted, "Call off your dog!"

I whirled around. MacDuff was circling the old woman, his fur bristling as his yellow eyes stared her down.

"Git *down*, MacDuff." I tried to make my voice deep like Grandfather's. MacDuff crouched in front of her, growling low in his chest. "Stay," I said. He froze where he was, his head following her movements as if she were some old ewe he'd cornered.

The woman walked toward us, breathing hard. "Your dog wouldn't let me in my shelter. I had to trick him, give him a cracker so I could catch him and tie him up. I was afraid he'd hurt the lamb."

"He knows not to do that," I said, and then shut my mouth tight. I wasn't sure I wanted to talk to this woman about anything, although the more I watched her, the more I was sure she was just a lonely old lady, not a ghost. And there was something about her that prickled in my mind. I felt as if I were trying to solve an easy math problem, but I'd forgotten how to add and subtract.

She picked up the length of rope, looped it over her elbow, then around her hand, winding it up.

"That's the rope from Grandfather's flagpole," I whispered.

"Correct." She dropped the coiled rope on the ground; Ginny reached down and scooped it up, stuffing it into her coat pocket.

The lamb nuzzled at my shirt. "It's hungry," I said.

The woman pointed at the spruce tree. A silver milk can was leaning up against the trunk. "There's plenty of milk for another feeding. I bought some on the mainland this morning—"

"Are you the ghost?" Ginny blurted.

The woman's head swiveled toward my sister. Her eyes were as big and watchful as an old tomcat's. "The ghost?" She actually smiled, showing black gaps where she was missing teeth. "I suppose you might say that—in a way."

Ginny edged close to me but I hardly noticed; I was staring at the frizzy braid coiled on the woman's head. What was it Grandfather had said last night— *Very small and dainty, . . . wore a long brown braid wrapped around her head . . .*

Suddenly everything made sense. "I know who you are," I said, holding the lamb close to help me feel brave.

"Is that so?" The old woman's voice was harsh and jagged, like a piece of broken glass.

I took a deep breath, but my voice still quivered.

"You're the dairymaid," I said. "The story's wrong. You sing that song about Delia being dead, but she's not. She didn't drown." I bit my lip. "*You're* Delia, aren't you?" I whispered.

For a minute, no one said a word. The hair on the back of my neck prickled when the old woman's head hunched into her shoulders like a bird. She glared at me, then sank onto a big rock, her skirts flapping around her. "You're right."

I let out my breath in a whoosh. The woman folded her hands in her lap. She had a funny, flat way of talking; you couldn't tell if she was angry or tired, or if she just didn't care about anything. "How did you figure it?" she asked.

"The song you sang, with your name in it. And Grandfather's story—he said you were very small, with a long braid on top of your head—"

Delia touched her grizzly hair and her eyes narrowed. "What does your Grandfather know about me?"

My tongue felt dry and thick, as if I'd just been to the dentist. "He tells this story—about a girl who grew up on the island and drowned. He scared us by saying her ghost still walks the breakwater. . . ." I glanced at Ginny, thinking how freaked we'd both been this morning.

"She was in love, too," Ginny said.

Delia frowned. "That so?"

"Some people even call this place 'Ghost Island' because of you," I added.

The old woman's mouth twitched. She seemed to like that idea.

"What are you doing here?" Ginny demanded. She was never the type that beats around the bush.

The woman called Delia swept her arm around the clearing, then made a big loop in the air, as if she were taking in the whole island. "What does it look like? I've come home."

11

Homeless

No one knew what to say for a minute. Finally Ginny licked her lips, and I could almost see ideas bouncing around inside her head. "This island belongs to some people called Hawkins now. Grandfather rents it from them."

The old woman smoothed her skirt, although it was so smudged and wrinkled I didn't know why she bothered. "I won't stay long," she said. "I'm just an old Gypsy."

Gypsy? Weren't they people who moved around in caravans a long time ago?

"Are you homeless?" Ginny asked.

Gol-ly, I thought, won't Ginny ever learn to be polite? But the old woman didn't seem to mind; she just shrugged her shoulders. "Some people might see it that way—your grandfather, for instance, or

85

the folks that own the island. When you move from place to place and job to job—then home is where you sleep at night. On the ground, under a bridge or in a dory, a barn or a shed—I've tried them all. Never stayed long in a real house, though. Not since I left." She looked around, her eyes dulled by the fog. "Some places are more home than others," she added quietly.

I thought of the homeless shelter in Portland. Our mom sings there sometimes, trying to cheer people up. One night last winter Ginny and I went with her. My mom played the kinds of songs everyone knows, but only a few people sang along. The rest of them just ate their supper or stared at my mom with these blank looks. Mom didn't mind; she said they were probably too sad or tired to sing.

"Do you ever sleep in shelters?" Ginny asked. She must have remembered the same thing.

The old woman stood up quickly. "Don't even mention that word," she warned. "A shelter's like a jail to me. I tried it once. Never again; not if I have a choice."

"Why did you come back to Lost Island?" Ginny asked.

"Let's just say I'm here to say good-bye," Delia said in her flat voice.

My mouth went dry; I remembered the old

cemetery. "Did you put those flowers on your own grave?" I whispered.

"So you found that, too," she said. "Nosy, aren't you."

When I didn't answer, she said, "Guess you didn't notice the dates on the stone. It's my grandmother who's buried there, not me. She was Delia Simpson, too. I was going to clean up my parents' graves as well, until you cluttered the island with your machinery and your dog."

I reached one hand up around the lamb so I could bite my thumbnail, and Ginny unwrapped another stick of gum and shoved it in her mouth, chewing nervously. "Grandfather said to be back before dark," she reminded me.

Delia held out a small, wizened hand, all crisscrossed with lines. "I could use a stick."

Ginny opened her mouth, then closed it again, reaching into her pocket. "Here," she said, handing her the whole pack, "you take it. I'm not supposed to chew it anyway, with my braces."

Even though she looked like a tiny gnome, this old woman sure had my sister jumping. Delia pocketed the gum without unwrapping any of it.

The lamb struggled in my arms. He was getting heavy. "May we feed him?" I asked.

"Grandfather's probably got a bottle," Ginny said. "Let's take him back to the cabin."

The old woman showed her teeth. "There's plenty of milk to feed him right here—I made sure of that this morning, when I crossed to the mainland. What's your hurry, girl?"

Ginny didn't answer. Delia reached into a deep pocket of her skirt and pulled out a blue rubber finger. "You'd be surprised what you find on the beach here, when you need things. Cut this off a glove that turned up at high tide, and poked a few holes in it." She disappeared into the shelter.

"Gabe, let's go." Ginny tugged my arm. "Grandfather said to be back before dark. And she's a nut," she added in a whisper.

"It's not dark yet. Hold on a minute." I wondered how things ever got so mixed up that *I* was trying to reassure my sister. I have to admit, I was really curious about this old lady. I'd never met anyone like her before.

Delia came back carrying an empty soda bottle and a piece of paper. "This will go faster if you help me." She glanced at Ginny, then me, waiting. Finally, Ginny held the bottle while Delia twisted the paper into a funnel and poured in milk from the jug. When the bottle was full, Delia stretched the cutoff finger over the top, holding it tight with a rubber band. "He'd like it better warm, but I don't dare make a fire. Someone might see it." She gave me the bottle.

I stared stupidly until I realized she was expecting me to feed the lamb. I lugged the baby to a flat place and sat down awkwardly, trying to get him comfortable in my lap.

At first, he couldn't find the nipple. He brushed it with his nose, then bleated. Ginny grabbed the bottle. "Gaby, you don't know what you're doing. Tip it up."

"Let them learn together." The old woman's voice was almost soothing now. She leaned over, tickled the lamb's tail, and squeezed a few drops of milk onto his pink tongue. His eyes rolled and his mouth searched for the nipple again. He tugged, then sucked, and when he finally began nursing, his long, scraggly tail twitched and wiggled. I smiled and settled back against a tree trunk. The baby was warm and heavy against my chest.

"What happened to the mother?" Ginny asked.

"She's dead." Delia wiped her hands on her skirt. "I did what I could, but I was too late. The old thing was almost gone when I found her. Guess the birth was too difficult."

"Where is she now?" Ginny asked.

Delia pointed toward the field, and I remembered the foul smell. "In the bushes. I tried to cover her a bit, to protect her from scavengers. Luckily, I was able to get some colostrum from the bag before she was gone."

"How'd you know about colostrum?" Ginny asked. She was sure being nosy, but I have to admit, I was glad she kept asking all these questions.

"We had sheep out here once," Delia answered, "so I knew babies need their mother's first milk."

It sounded like Delia had a soft spot for animals—like me. I shifted on the hard ground, feeling uncomfortable all over. One minute, Delia had scared me half to death. The next second she seemed—well, not normal, but not really crazy either.

The lamb finished the bottle, dropped the nipple, and snuggled up to me. His ears twitched when I whispered, "You're going to be all right." His tightly curled black fleece was like my own hair. He could be my animal twin.

I glanced at Ginny. Usually, when I bring home some wounded thing—a bird with a broken wing, or the runt of a litter of kittens—she complains. "Not *another* one," she'll say. But this time, her eyes were soft, too. I guess even Ginny couldn't abandon an orphan lamb.

"Gabe, let's go," Ginny hissed.

"Wait." The woman stepped close to us, and I stood up carefully, holding my breath. "Who's your grandfather?"

I hesitated. He was always just "Grandfather" to me, but Ginny said quickly: "Evan. Evan O'Day."

"O'Day." Delia thought a minute. "Kevin's boy," she said at last. "He was just a little squirt when I left home."

Ginny and I glanced at each other. It was funny to think of Grandfather, who was so tall and rangy, being a "little squirt."

Delia poked me in the arm. "Don't you have a name?"

"Gabriel," I gulped. Just when I thought she was all right, she spooked me again.

"I'm Virginia," Ginny said in a stiff voice. "And we're leaving now. Oh no—Gabriel, where's MacDuff?"

How could we have missed him? MacDuff had disappeared again. Suddenly, we heard Grandfather's whistle, all lonely in the fog, and then MacDuff's frantic yelps. It sounded as if they were far away, but it was hard to tell; the fog made everything seem muffled. I was about to halloo back at them, but Delia closed her knobby fingers around my wrist.

"Quiet. I don't want them to find me here."

"How come?" I asked nervously, jerking my hand away. Maybe she *was* some kind of nut after all.

"Like as not they'd think I need help. Not that I blame them. After all, I do make people nervous."

You could say that again! Delia was moving quickly around the clearing now, picking things up as if she were tidying her living room. She pulled on a faded wool coat with a hood. "An old lady living outside alone, they think it's a kindness to offer her a bed in a nursing home, maybe even a mental hospital." Her voice was small and her shoulders sagged under the heavy coat. All of a sudden, I wasn't afraid of her anymore. She was just a frightened old lady; a little weird, but not scary. I felt light inside, as if a big space had opened up in the fog and I could see forever.

But Ginny obviously had other ideas. She put her hands on her hips and demanded, "If you're so worried about getting caught, why didn't you leave this morning? We saw you going across the breakwater."

Delia reached out and rubbed the lamb's forehead. "Truth is, I couldn't abandon this little fellow. He needed milk to survive, so I fetched it for him. I was glad to see I could still carry a can of milk across after all these years. . . ." Her voice drifted away in wisps, like the fog all around us. "I never planned to come back here," she said. "Avoided the place for almost sixty years. Then I found myself near Stone Harbor and realized there was still a piece of business I needed to tidy up on the island."

She made it sound as if she had to go to a lawyer's office. What was she talking about? The lamb shivered and I felt the same way inside. "So Grandfather's story is true," I said. "You took the milk to the dairy every day—"

"And you had a boyfriend, right?" Ginny blurted.

Good grief. Couldn't she forget that romance stuff, even for a minute? But Delia's eyes actually brightened a tiny bit. "*Boyfriend*," she mocked. "In those days, he was called my 'young man.' But he's gone now," she added after a little pause, and I almost expected her to start singing her creepy song again.

"Did you come back to the island because of him?" Ginny didn't look suspicious anymore; her face had this dreamy look, the one she gets when she's reading one of those boring romance novels she drools over.

"Yes and no," Delia said. She straightened her shoulders. "There's no time to lose now—your grandfather may come this way." She handed Ginny the milky soda bottle and the nipple, stooped to pick up the milk cans, and said to me, "Can you manage the lamb? As I said, I have one thing to clear up here on the island—and I could use your help. It won't take long."

"We have to go back," Ginny said. She was starting to sound like a windup doll that only says one thing.

Delia stared her down. "If you want to know more about Jack, I suggest you come with me."

"Jack?" Ginny actually froze in her tracks. Her eyes flickered. "Was that your boyfriend's name—I mean, your 'young man'?"

Delia didn't answer. She fixed her tiny eyes on me, and I had the feeling she thought she knew me from somewhere else. "What about you, boy?" she said. "You're game to help me, aren't you?"

"I guess," I stuttered.

Delia rummaged in her pockets—how many did she have, anyway?—and pulled out my flashlight. "Belong to either of you?"

"It's mine." I gripped the lamb tightly with one arm and took the flashlight back. "Thanks, but—"

"You and your sister will need it later. The place we're going, I could find my way blindfolded."

I wanted to ask where that was, but Ginny yanked my arm. "Grandfather's coming this way."

"Then it's time to be gone." Delia stood so close to Ginny their faces nearly touched and my sister actually flinched. "You decide, girl. Come with me, and find out how much truth there is in your grandfather's story—or go back to the cabin alone, if you're too afraid. Me and Gabriel here have work to do."

Her voice was as dark and spooky as the shadows under the spruce trees. Ginny scowled, and I knew Delia had hit the right buttons. No one tells Ginny she's afraid and gets away with it. Before Ginny

could blurt out something she'd regret, I said
quickly, "Grandfather told us you drowned crossing
the breakwater."

She looked pleased. "Sounds like he spins the
yarn I intended."

I licked my lips. "You mean—you faked it?"

Delia didn't answer. She picked up her heavy
pack and started out of the clearing. "We'll take the
beach trail to my old house," she called over her
shoulder. "No talking until we get there." She
buttoned her coat, gave us one last look, and started
for the field.

"Come on, Gin," I said, "she's talking about the
cellar hole, I bet—that's close to the cabin. We can
always leave."

Ginny frowned, then said, "Okay—but as soon as
she tells us the story, we're out of there—right?"

"Right." We plunged into the woods after Delia.
Her shadow was just ahead, weaving in and out of
the spruces. I clutched the lamb to my chest,
tucking his head under my arm so the branches
wouldn't whip his eyes. "Hold tight, little one," I
whispered. "We're off on a crazy adventure—but it
will all be over soon."

12

Jack

When we came out of the trees into the meadow, the wet grass soaked Ginny's and my pants immediately. The fog was so thick now, I didn't think anyone would see us, but Delia took a winding path, cutting across the field and down toward the water—I guess she didn't want us near the cabin.

Everything was quiet; even the waves whispered, as though Delia had managed to keep them from talking, too. We couldn't hear Grandfather or MacDuff anymore. Delia sure moved fast; she might be small and old but we had to hurry to keep up. The lamb seemed heavier and heavier; my legs dragged and I had a blister on my heel. I glanced behind me to see if Ginny was following. She rolled her eyes at me but she looked more cheerful, almost excited. I felt a little better.

We walked along the top of the beach because the tide was high. When we passed the graveyard, I gave Ginny a nudge, pointing. She craned her neck to see in, but I kept on going. I didn't care *whose* graves they were, I didn't want to hang around in that spooky fog.

Delia never said a word until we reached the cellar hole, and then she disappeared so quickly I thought she might have fallen in. I ran to the edge and turned on the flashlight, peering down. Delia was waiting quietly; she looked small and square under the old coat. "Bring the lamb with you," she said. "He'll be safe."

But would *we* be safe down there with her? Ginny and I glanced at each other. "Come on," Delia said, "I won't bite. And if I can't find it right away, you can leave."

Find what? Now I was curious, too. "You go first," I said to Ginny. "I'll hand the lamb down to you."

"Thanks a bunch," Ginny said, but she scrambled down the wall ahead of me. When we were all settled in the cellar of the old house, Delia said, "I could use that light now." I gave her my flashlight without thinking; she turned it on and swept her arm around the foundation. "Hard to believe this was once my home. The cookstove was just above us here." She turned slowly, like someone playing blindman's buff, then aimed the light into a dark corner. "The root cellar was over there—where we stored potatoes, carrots, and parsnips. Terrible things, parsnips."

"Where did you sleep?" Ginny asked.

"Upstairs—all in one room. And the roof leaked right onto our beds."

My sister's eyes were bright; I bet she liked imagining where all the rooms were and what the house looked like.

"What are you looking for?" I asked.

Delia pushed past the little birch tree that grew right out of the floor, and went to the jumbled chimney.

"Something I left behind about sixty years ago," she explained with a strange little laugh. "Pretty foolish to think it'd be waiting for me." She turned the light on the chimney and stared. "Someone's been here already," she said, pointing to the names.

"What is it?" Ginny bent over. "Julia, Tom—" she said slowly, spelling them out. "Who are these people?"

"I found them this morning," I said. "Were they your brothers and sisters?" I asked Delia.

She nodded, studying me again. "You've done a lot of figuring, haven't you?" She traced her fingers over the letters and sighed. "My family. There are ghosts everywhere," she muttered. I looked around nervously, and she showed us her funny smile. "Just a manner of speaking," she explained. "Memories bring people back, as if they were ghosts. . . ."

She gave me the flashlight and raised her arms to her shoulders, touching the wall lightly. "Now, what I'm looking for is somewhere right here—I remember it was about shoulder height. We'll need to pull the chimney apart, I'm afraid." She took hold of a loose stone, rocking it back and forth until it fell to the ground, just missing her foot; then she reached her arm into the open hole and shook her head. "Not there—it wasn't such a big stone, anyway; at least, not as I remember it. Still, it was a long time ago. . . ." Her voice was drifting like someone falling asleep.

"What are you looking for?" I asked again.

"A box," Delia said. "It had some letters in it—"

"*Letters?*" Ginny squealed. She poked me in the ribs and nodded toward Delia as if she'd just turned into the world's most interesting person. "Were they letters from your boyfriend—from Jack?"

"That's right." Delia's small hands worked around in the crevices like a coon searching for food. "I kept them hidden down here, so my parents wouldn't find them. They didn't like Jack much, which was smart, now that I look back on it."

Ginny and I glanced at each other. Delia kept giving us these little hints, as if we were on a treasure hunt together, but then she'd stop talking, leaving us with no clues to follow.

"Come on," Delia snapped. "You can pull out some stones—or hold the light for me. It will go faster that way."

So I aimed the light while Ginny and Delia took the chimney apart, stone by stone. When the rocks were too heavy, we lowered them to the floor together. In a few minutes, we had a small pile on the ground; once, a big rock tumbled onto the heap, scaring the lamb. I picked him up quickly, petted him, and set him down again. It was getting darker every minute, and I wondered if Grandfather would be worried about us.

Delia had her hand on a smooth, round rock, bigger than my fist. She gave it to Ginny, then stuck her hand into the hole and pulled out a wooden box with a metal latch, the kind our grandmother uses for recipe cards. "Well, what do you know," Delia whispered. The box was mildewed and dusty; she wiped it on her skirt, then slipped it into a deep coat pocket without even opening it.

I thought my sister would pop. "Aren't you going to look inside?" Ginny gasped.

"When the time comes," Delia said.

"But how do you know the letters are still in there?" Ginny wailed.

"Gee, Gin, take it easy," I said. "It's her box."

Delia brushed my sister's questions away as if she were a mosquito buzzing around. "Something's inside," she said. "If it's not the letters, so be it."

"Won't you *please* tell us about Jack," Ginny begged, her voice all sweet and sugary. "You said you would."

Delia hesitated, then sat down on a big rock. "There's not much to tell—it was just like any other romance. A young woman falls in love for the first time—and then the man turns out to be different than her dream of him."

Ginny frowned. She likes love stories to have a happy ending, but she sat down near Delia anyway, hugging her knees. I took the lamb in my lap, cuddling up to his warmth.

"Where did you meet him?" Ginny asked.

"At the dairy." Delia's face turned toward the mainland as though she could still see the building. "Living on the island, so isolated after my brothers and sisters left, I didn't know many young people. The first time I saw Jack, lifting milk cans from the wagon, I was smitten." She leaned toward me, and I tried not to pull away from her dank, sour smell. "Bet you don't use that word now—'smitten.' It means you see someone special who makes your heart quake; you get all shaky inside."

My heart sure quaked and shook when I first saw Delia, but I knew that wasn't what she meant. I glanced at Ginny. She was listening to the old woman with dreamy eyes, lapping up her story like a cat.

"Jack was a handsome young man, with black curly hair," Delia went on. She took my flashlight and turned it full in my face until I had to duck my head. "First time I saw you, boy, you gave me quite a turn. Thought you were a young Jack, come back to haunt me." I flinched and she laughed a little. "Don't like all this talk about ghosts, do you?"

I shook my head. I'd had enough ghosts on this trip to last me a lifetime.

"Anyway, before long Jack and I were courting. My father was surprised; for years he'd prodded me to take the milk to town; now I wanted to go every day, even when we didn't have much. Sometimes, I'd walk across and Jack would be gone; he had to collect the milk from farms up and down the coast. That's when he'd leave me notes. They were pretty things, sweet as molasses cookies. Jack was well educated; he could persuade you of anything with his words—on paper, or when he talked."

Ginny looked longingly at Delia's pocket, and I almost laughed out loud. I bet her dumb romance books weren't half as good as this story.

"We courted all through the fall and winter. When the fall rains came, I rowed across the bay. In winter, during the worst weather, my father took the milk, but Jack would slip a note in the empty cans, after he'd drained them. My father brought the letters home without knowing—I'd find them when I washed out the cans."

Delia's face was softer, as though telling the story was making her young again. "Jack said we'd be married in the summer, when he could save up some money and take a few days off. Then one day—it was about this time of year, when things were greening and the cows had freshened—"

She stopped suddenly, holding up her hand. "Listen."

"Don't stop the story now!" Ginny gasped.

Delia jumped to her feet and cocked her head. This time we all heard it. "Gaaabe! Ginny!" Uncle Paul was calling our names; it sounded as if he was up at the cabin.

"Be off now, both of you," Delia said, shooing us away. She looked angry; the spell was broken.

"He won't find us," Ginny protested. "Please, tell us the rest. Please!"

Delia gave me the flashlight, hoisted her pack, and climbed out of the cellar hole, glaring down at Ginny from above. "Jack jilted me," she hissed. "You can figure out the rest on your own."

"How!" Ginny cried.

I nudged her. "Come on, let's get out of here. Do you want to get her in trouble?"

Ginny pouted, then clenched her fists. "It's not fair," she complained, but she climbed out anyway. Typical, I thought. First she bosses me around in the clearing, saying it's time to go; now she's hooked on Delia and doesn't want to leave. I had to admit, Delia's story *was* pretty interesting; I wanted to know the ending, too, but she didn't look as if she were going to tell us anything more. Her mouth made a straight, thin line above her pointy chin.

"Not a word about any of this," Delia snapped when we were all standing on top of the wall. "Don't say anything about me to your grandfather. I'll only be here a few more days, at the most—you can see I'm not hurting anything."

"Come with us!" Ginny said suddenly. "Grandfather will help you—I'm sure he would!"

Delia shook her head. "I don't need his kind of help. Get away now, before he sees me."

"Where will you go?" I asked, and then, before she could answer, I had an idea. "You can hide in that little shed, by the shearing pens. It's full of wool bags. You can sleep on the fleeces, and no one will see you in there."

She raised her hand. "Thanks," she said, "I might just do that."

"Will we see you tomorrow?" Ginny asked, but Delia took two steps into the fog and disappeared.

I grabbed my sister before she could run after Delia. "Come on, Ginny, let's get out of here. We've got some 'figuring' to do, as Delia would say."

Ginny dragged her feet behind me. The dark dropped over us like a heavy quilt as we groped our way up the hill. Even with my flashlight on, it was hard to see, but someone had lit a fire in the cabin and we followed the smell of smoke. I felt really tired. The lamb's legs knocked against me, and Ginny and I kept bumping into each other.

"Watch out," Ginny complained. "Gabe, she must be so lonely."

"Maybe." I couldn't tell what Delia felt about anything. "Listen, Gin, you read those dumb love stories all the time—what does 'jilted' mean?"

"They're not dumb stories. And if you read them, you'd know what it means: Jack left her. Maybe he ran away before the wedding, or he told her he didn't love her anymore. Poor Delia." She gave such a long, deep sigh, you'd think *she* was the one Jack had ditched.

"Listen," I said, stepping close so I could see into her eyes. "We can't tell Grandfather about her."

"But he could help her," Ginny protested.

"You heard Delia—she doesn't want to be helped. She saved the lamb," I said, giving him a little squeeze. "And she's not doing anything wrong. Grandfather will tell her she's trespassing and make her leave the island. She'll only be here a few more days. The Hawkinses don't have to know. Besides, it's her island—in a way."

For once, Ginny agreed with me. "All right. But if we get in trouble, don't blame me."

"I won't," I said, but I had a heavy feeling in my stomach. If Grandfather asked us questions, it wouldn't be so easy to hide everything. We decided to tell him the truth about finding the lamb in the shelter—but we'd pretend we didn't know how it got there.

In another minute, the porch railings appeared out of nowhere, and a soft light glowed from the windows of the cabin.

"Halloo!" Ginny called. The door opened and Uncle Paul stepped out, holding another lantern over his head. When we yelled at him again, his whole face seemed to grin.

"Boy, you two sure had me worried." He peered beyond us into the dark. "Your granddad's not with you?"

We hurried onto the porch. "We heard Grandfather whistling, and MacDuff barking," I said. "I think he'll be here soon. Uncle Paul, look what we found."

He stared. "Well, I'll be—what have we got here?"

"A newborn lamb."

He looked at me, then at Ginny. "Aren't you something. Come on inside now and get warm. I can see we've got a lot of talking to do."

13

Like a Bear in a Cage

We followed Uncle Paul into the cabin. It was warm and cozy; onions sizzled in a frying pan and a fire popped in the stove. I set the lamb on the floor inside the door. His legs wobbled, but this time he was able to stand without falling down. Uncle Paul hung the lantern on a hook and scooped the lamb up under his arm, talking to it gently. "A little ram lamb. Born too early, weren't you? Where was he hiding?" he asked us.

Ginny and I glanced at each other. "Um—up on the hill—in the woods," she stammered.

"Where's the mother?"

I gulped. "I—I don't know. The lamb was in that shelter I found yesterday, all by itself. Do you think the mother might be lost?"

Uncle Paul shook his head. "I doubt it. Someone's fed him well, otherwise he'd be too weak to stand."

I gave Ginny a desperate look, but she just shrugged.

Uncle Paul pulled on his boots. "Where are you going?" I asked quickly.

"To find Pop. He's been out there too long, stubborn old fool." I knew Uncle Paul didn't mean that about Grandfather; he was just worried.

"MacDuff was barking up on the hill." My words came out in a rush. "Then we heard Grandfather whistling—I'm sure they're up near the shelter."

"Yeah, up that way," Ginny said, waving her arm in the opposite direction from the shearing pens.

"Why didn't you call to him?" Uncle Paul asked, zipping his coat.

"We did!" Ginny didn't even blush when she lied. "We yelled our heads off, but he didn't hear us," she added.

To our relief, Uncle Paul chuckled. "I'm not surprised. His hearing's pretty bad. Doesn't like to admit it, though." He took the lantern from the table, looping the wire over his arm. "There's another lamp lit in the kitchen. Could you two work on supper? Add ground meat to the onions, and toss the spaghetti in the pot when the water boils. I'll be back shortly."

He was gone before we could say anything else;

the lantern bobbed and swung along the path and then dissolved in the foggy dark.

Ginny and I looked at each other, then at the lamb. "Boy, that was close," she said.

"Yeah. But it might not be so easy with Grandfather."

She waggled her hips from side to side. "We'll see. Grandfather always believes me."

I stared. "You mean, you've lied to him before?"

She squinted. "What do you think? Not big lies, of course."

I couldn't remember *ever* lying to Grandfather, and the thought made me feel sick.

Ginny took off her jacket. "Don't worry, Gabe; we'll fake it somehow. Come on, let's make dinner. Uncle Paul told you to help, too."

"I will. Just let me make a place for the lamb."

I pulled off my boots while the lamb took a few delicate steps around the room, exploring. I decided to make him a bed in the woodbox. I took out the driftwood logs and stacked them near the door, then folded an old sheepskin and cuddled my face against the lamb's warm belly before settling him in his new bed. His fleece was as dark as the potbellied stove ticking beside us. "Cinders," I whispered in his ear, "that's your name." He curled up tight in a corner and fell asleep.

"I can't stop thinking about Delia's story," Ginny

said. "It sounds like she faked her drowning, on purpose. We'll have to find her in the morning, somehow, and get her to tell us the rest." She started giving me orders about dinner, but I just let them drift past me. I stirred the meat when she dumped it into the skillet, then put plates and glasses on the table. It had started to rain; water drummed gently on the tin roof. I couldn't keep Delia out of my mind either. It didn't seem fair for her to get cold and wet when we had this cozy cabin to sleep in. I felt guilty, nibbling on grated cheese and breathing in the steamy smell of meat and onions cooking, while she was out there in the dark with nothing but my sister's gum in her pockets.

Ginny dumped a box of spaghetti in the pot, jumping as hot water spattered the stove, and then deep voices boomed, the lantern light shone in the doorway, and Grandfather came in, leaning on Uncle Paul's arm. His face was as white as his hair.

I ran to him. "Grandfather—what's wrong?"

He grunted, settled himself in a chair, and pulled off his cap. "I took a spill in the woods—nothing to worry about." He coughed, then looked from Ginny to me.

"Paul tells me you found a little critter out there."

I nodded, pointing at the woodbox. "His name is Cinders," I said.

"Since when?" Ginny asked, but I didn't answer; I was watching Grandfather.

"Bring him here," he said, and then added quickly, "if you please. I'm too tired to move another inch."

I set the lamb in Grandfather's lap. He held him up, looking at his tummy, then let him skitter across the floor, his sharp hooves clicking. MacDuff had flopped down on the sheepskin rug, but his yellow eyes never left the lamb.

"Shouldn't we feed him?" I asked.

Grandfather nodded. "We'll mix up some powdered milk in a minute. Right now we've got some talking to do." He set his cap on the table. His saggy cheeks were stubbly; he hadn't shaved since we'd been on the island.

"MacDuff led me to the mother," he said. "Matter of fact, I fell right over her." He rubbed his knee, wincing a little. "You were right, Paul—I've no business roaming around in the dark, even with a light. Anyway, someone's obviously given this lamb some help. Cut the cord on its belly, fed it, too." His blue eyes settled on me. "I found the shelter you told me about. Wish I'd listened to you yesterday. Maybe we'd have straightened all this out earlier. Right now, there's no sign anyone was there. Those blankets and cans you told me about are gone."

I glanced at Ginny. What now?

Grandfather was waiting. "I don't want to frighten you kids, but I'm worried about prowlers on the island. Since we hadn't seen a boat, I figured they'd left, but now I'm not so sure. Where'd you find the lamb?"

I cleared my throat. "He was in the shelter."

"Just sitting there?" Grandfather's voice was tired.

"MacDuff was guarding him—" I began, stalling.

Grandfather scratched his head, puzzled, and looked at Uncle Paul. "I can't figure it. It's not like Duffer to ignore us when we call. He must have heard my whistle."

I opened my mouth, then shut it again. Grandfather reached into the pocket of his pants, pulling out the coiled rope and something else—a long red scarf. He set the rope on the table. "This came off my flagpole. I found it up by the shelter. Did you see it when you were up there?"

Ginny and I both squirmed and Grandfather's eyebrows drew together over his eyes.

"I had the rope in my pocket," Ginny said at last. "I guess—I must have dropped it."

Grandfather put one rough hand on Ginny's arm, the other on mine. "Come on, kids. Any fool could see you're hiding something." He took a deep breath. "Out with it. I'm sure you haven't done anything wrong, but if you hide the truth, then there will be consequences to pay."

I swallowed hard. Grandfather held up the scarf. It was gauzy and worn, although it looked as if it had once been fancy. I was surprised by the color; it was so bright compared to everything else Delia wore.

"And who do you suppose dropped this on the ground," Grandfather asked. His blue eyes were cold, and I knew he was getting angry. I couldn't stand that.

"The scarf might belong to an old woman," I whispered, glancing quickly at Ginny. Her face looked as hot as mine. "The same old lady who used your rope to tie MacDuff to a tree."

Grandfather tipped his head to the side as if he hadn't heard me right. "Old woman?"

"She was taking care of the lamb." I was talking slowly, but my mind was racing ahead, trying to think of how to tell him just a little without giving Delia away completely. "She saved his life. She even went to the mainland to buy milk—"

"Hold it a minute." Grandfather put up his hand. "Let's start at the beginning. You met this person? Who is she?"

My eyes met Ginny's. We were each waiting for the other one to start. Finally I couldn't stand it anymore. When it comes to Grandfather getting mad, I guess I'm still a coward. "She asked us not to tell," I said, blinking fast.

Grandfather gripped the edge of the table with his fingers. The knuckles were scratched and raw and his long steady stare made my heart beat faster. "Do you think that's a good idea?" he asked in a quiet but scary voice. "Not telling?"

"No," I whispered.

I waited, but Ginny only said, "Go on, Gabe, you might as well get it over with."

I took a deep breath. "She's the dairymaid, the one in the story." When no one spoke, I said, "Her name is Delia Simpson."

Grandfather's mouth twitched as if he might laugh. "Now, Gabriel, I can't imagine—" he began, but Uncle Paul put his hand on Grandfather's shoulder.

"Hold on, Pop, let him talk."

Slowly, a little bit at a time, I explained about finding signs of Delia in the grapevine house, the gravestone, and the names in the cellar hole, although I didn't tell them about going there with her. I didn't want them to know she might be close by.

"We thought she was the ghost at first," Ginny said. "We saw her on the breakwater and she looked really spooky, just like in your story." She laced up her fingers and pushed them together until they popped. "But then Gabriel figured out who she was."

She gave me a shy smile, like she might even be impressed with me for once. Amazing. I was so surprised, I drew myself up nice and tall.

Grandfather pulled on his ear. "Sounds like you discovered a lot." He studied me for a minute, his forehead wrinkling.

Uncle Paul crossed his arms over his chest. "Whew," he said, "who would have thought that old coot was still alive?" He laughed, but stopped when he saw the frown on Grandfather's face. "What's the matter, Pop?"

Grandfather looked at us, then at Uncle Paul, the way grown-ups do when they've decided to discuss something after the kids are asleep. "I've got to think about all this a minute." He picked up his hat, tossed it across the room, and said in a kind of fake, hearty voice, "Say, it smells pretty good in here—what's for dinner?"

"The spaghetti!" Ginny yelped and ran to the stove with Uncle Paul right behind her. Grandfather got up slowly, and put his big hand on my head, flattening my curls. "You've done a good job today, Gabriel," he said in a gruff voice, and I felt a little glow, as if someone had taken hot coals from the fire and set them against my heart. "I believe what you've told me, and I appreciate how you'd think this woman might be Delia Simpson," he said carefully. "But I'm afraid she's putting you on. How old do you think she is?"

"Pretty old," I said. "Older than you."

"Really ancient," he snorted, his eyes twinkling.

"She remembers you," I insisted. "She knew you were Kevin O'Day's son."

Grandfather looked surprised, but he just said, "Huh. Well, I suppose that could be some kind of coincidence."

"I *know* she's Delia." My eyes were hot and I rubbed them quickly. I thought of how she only wanted a few more days on her island. Now we'd spoiled it for her.

"Well, we'll see. In any case, she did us a favor, rescuing this critter. Let's give him some dinner."

He helped me mix up some powdered milk for Cinders, using warm water from the kettle near the stove. While I fed the lamb, Grandfather took off his boots, wriggled his toes, and settled back in the rocking chair. The lamb tugged on the nipple; he was standing up to nurse now, stretching his neck out.

"What about the lamb, Grandfather—can we keep him?"

Grandfather opened his eyes and cocked his head to the side. "It's a big job, keeping a little one warm and fed. He'll need four or five feedings a day at first—think you're up to it?"

"I'll do it," I said. "I promise." I rubbed my hand along the lamb's side. His belly was swelling with the milk.

Grandfather grunted. "A ram can't be a pet forever, or he becomes a nuisance. But if he grows nicely, we could bring him back to the island this fall; turn him out with the ewes. He might father some nice lambs."

You're safe, Cinders, I thought, and grinned. Dishes clinked around the corner; Uncle Paul and Ginny laughed. It was cozy and warm here—if only I could forget about Delia being outside.

"Listen to that rain," Grandfather said. "I don't like to imagine anyone outdoors on a night like this. You don't have any idea where she might be holed up, do you?"

"Ah—I'm not sure," I said, keeping my eyes on the lamb. The least I could do was protect Delia tonight. We'd think of something else by morning. "She said she could find her way around the island blindfolded."

"Well, I suppose she'll locate some kind of shelter—and she's probably used to it, poor thing. We'll look for her after dinner. Of course, we'll have to take her to shore in the morning; get her settled somewhere."

I bit my lip. "Like where?"

Grandfather reached over and ruffled my hair. "Don't worry, Gabriel, we'll find a nice place for her. Whoever she is, she shouldn't be wandering around out here alone, not at her age." He grinned at me. "I'm a fine one to talk, eh? Now put that lamb to bed and wash your hands."

I rinsed my hands in the bucket by the front door. It was turning out just the way Delia had said. I thought of a time when our parents took us to the zoo and I watched a polar bear pace up and down, its big paws padding and curling on the pavement as it followed the same path like a robot. Wouldn't Delia be like that bear in its cage, if they put her in some kind of home?

"Soup's on!" Uncle Paul called, coming around the corner with a steaming kettle of spaghetti. Ginny followed him with a loaf of bread and a plate of raw carrots. I set Cinders in his bed and glanced out the window into the blackness. I knew Grandfather was only trying to be nice, but Delia didn't want to be helped. And she certainly wasn't a "poor thing." What should we do? I scraped my chair close to the table. Pretty soon the hot spaghetti sliding down my throat made all my worries disappear—but only for a little while.

14

Escape from Lost Island

After dinner, Uncle Paul took the big red flashlight and went looking for Delia. Grandfather dozed in the rocking chair with his sore leg propped up on a crate. Ginny and I kept peering out the window as we washed the dishes, afraid Uncle Paul would come back with Delia, but all we saw were our own white faces reflected in the wet glass.

Uncle Paul wasn't gone long; he came in shaking his head. "Can't see a thing out there," he said. "She could be holed up anywhere. I have to assume she's all right—we'll keep looking in the morning."

Grandfather hoisted himself from his chair. "What about a radio call to the sheriff?" he asked. "We could ask him to come out first thing with a search party."

"The sheriff?" I asked in a squeaky voice. "What's she done wrong?"

Grandfather sighed. "Trespassing, for one thing. And I don't want an injured old lady on my hands; surely you can understand that. Gabriel, you and Virginia have done a fine job, but now it's time for us to take over."

Grandfather sounded like a typical grown-up, which made me mad. He wasn't usually like that. Luckily for Delia, Uncle Paul said, "Pop, I'm just too tired to go down to the boat now, and I hate to bother the sheriff so late. Let's see what tomorrow brings."

Grandfather grumbled, but he didn't argue. Ginny and I rolled out our sleeping bags near the stove and then she gave Cinders his last bottle. "He'll need a night feed," Grandfather said as he stoked the stove.

My mind raced. If I had an excuse to get up in the night, I might be able to warn Delia somehow—if I dared. "I'll do it," I said quickly.

"Help yourself," Ginny yawned, spreading the junk from her pack in a circle around her. "You know what I'm like in the middle of the night."

I set my watch for two o'clock and climbed into my bag. "Blow out the lamp when you're ready for bed," Grandfather said. He went into the little bedroom with Uncle Paul and shut the door.

Ginny lifted the glass, puffed on the flame until it died, then got into her bag. She settled down, but I could hear Grandfather murmuring to Uncle Paul. I inched across the floor in my sleeping bag and put my ear to the door, straining to hear what they were saying.

"Gabe!" Ginny hissed, "what are you doing?"

I waved at her to be quiet. "What do you think of Gabe's ghost story?" Uncle Paul asked. "Could this woman really be Delia Simpson?"

"It's possible," Grandfather answered. "Although she'd have to be nearly eighty. That's pretty old to be walking the breakwater."

"If she's still alive, Gabriel's sure made a mess of your story," Uncle Paul chuckled.

I held my breath, wondering what Grandfather would say. To my surprise, he laughed. "These kids will have their *own* stories to tell after this weekend." That's for sure, I thought. There was a slithering noise as Ginny crawled up beside me. Beds squeaked on the other side of the door; I could imagine Uncle Paul and Grandfather climbing in.

"I think we should take the kids home before we bring out a search party, in case there's trouble," Grandfather said. "From the sound of it, she probably belongs in a shelter, and I'd hate to get Gabe and Ginny mixed up in that."

How are we supposed to learn about the hard

things if the grown-ups always try to protect us? I wondered. Uncle Paul said something else, but I couldn't hear him, and Grandfather didn't answer.

That settles it, I thought, sliding back across the floor with Ginny beside me. We put our heads together near the stove.

"What should we do?" she whispered.

"I'm going to warn her when I get up with the lamb. There won't be time in the morning."

Ginny pulled her flashlight out of her pack and turned it on, cupping her hand over the end. "But, Gabe," she giggled, "you're afraid of the dark."

I shrugged. "So?"

Ginny shone the light in my eyes, making me wince. "Won't you be too scared?" she whispered.

"Probably." I dove down into my bag. She wasn't going to talk me out of it now.

I could hear Ginny's sigh even with my head buried. "You're sure acting different out here. Maybe Delia put a spell on you."

"That's enough chatter, kids," Grandfather called. "Go to sleep."

Ginny tugged the bag away from my head and put her mouth to my ear. "You can't go out there alone," she said softly. "I'm coming, too." Man, I thought, she's the only person I know who can sound bossy even when she's whispering. But I was really relieved that she wanted to come. Running around an island on a dark, rainy night was *not* my idea of a good time.

"You just want to hear the end of the story," I hissed.

"So what if I do? Wake me up," she said again.

"Okay," I whispered. "But you have to promise: no bossing me around."

"No problem," she said, snapping off the flashlight.

No problem? I bet we'd have quite a few problems before the night was over, but I was too tired to think about that now.

I dreamed I was lost at sea, trying to find my way back by following the foghorn, and woke up with my watch going breep, breep, breep! I turned on my flashlight and stumbled to my feet, tripping over Ginny in the dark. She didn't wake up; it would probably take a firecracker to budge her. Grandfather's steady snore rattled in the next room.

I warmed the milk and filled the bottle, sitting on my sleeping bag while Cinders nursed. He was wide awake, but I had to prop my other hand under my chin; I could hardly keep my eyes open.

When the lamb was done, I settled him in the woodbox and shone my flashlight on my cozy sleeping bag. It would be so easy to get back in. But then I thought of the sheriff and a bunch of people swarming over the island, chasing Delia as if she'd just escaped from jail. The least we could do was warn her.

I shook Ginny's shoulder. "Wha—?" she muttered. I clapped my hand over her mouth.

"Don't talk," I whispered. She inched out of her bag. It took us a few minutes to find our jackets, boots, and flashlights. I switched my light on for a second, found Delia's scarf on the table, and stuffed it into my pocket. As we opened the door, MacDuff's tail thumped; he was curled up near the lamb, guarding him. I'd feel safer if he came along, but I was afraid he'd bark.

"Stay," I said softly. "Good dog."

We slipped outside. The fog was gone but the island still seemed spooky with a big moon stretching long, silver shadows across the field. I led the way around the cabin and down the hill. We didn't say a word until we reached the pens. They were quiet and empty in the dark.

"What if she's not there?" Ginny whispered.

I shrugged and shone my light into the little shed. The bulging burlap sacks were heaped on top of each other and the smell of wool was strong. Nothing moved.

"Delia?" I whispered. The wool bag near my feet shifted and I recognized Delia's coat wedged between two sacks. She sat up slowly. Her long gray braid was dangling over one shoulder and her eyes were sunk deep into their wrinkled sockets. I felt embarrassed, as if we'd barged into her bedroom.

"Sorry," I said, "we had to warn you. Grandfather's going to organize a search party in the morning. He's talking about bringing the sheriff."

She raised her squirrelly face toward mine. "I told you not to tell him about me."

"We couldn't help it!" I cried, edging away. "Grandfather found the shelter, and the dead sheep. And the lamb was so healthy, he could tell someone had fed him. He figured it out." I couldn't admit that *we'd* told him everything else.

"But you decided to help me. Why?" Delia's eyes darted from Ginny to me like a bird.

"Grandfather talked about taking you to a shelter," I said, "and we knew you wouldn't like that."

Delia buttoned her coat across her chest; her fingers fumbled and shook. She glanced at the moon, dipping toward the mainland. "Far as I know, there's only one way for me to get off this island," she muttered and disappeared into the back of the shed. We waited for a few minutes. When she came back, her hair was twisted on top of her head again, and she was carrying her milk cans and backpack.

"Had a nice rest on those fleeces," she said with a sad smile. "Softest mattress I've had in months."

She turned toward the shore. "Guess I'll wait on the beach for the tide to turn. The breakwater should show by eight or so."

"But they'll see you! Grandfather's always up early!" I bit my nail so hard it broke with a snap. I breathed all the way into my stomach, knowing that once I'd said what I had to say, there'd be no turning back. "We can take you to shore in the boat."

Delia whirled around, squinting at me, and Ginny warned, "Gabe—we can't do that! It's too dangerous."

"No bossing," I reminded her in a low voice.

"Pay attention to your sister for once—she's right," Delia snapped at me. She stalked toward the dunes, holding her skirt above the wet grass. "You've got no business running a lobster boat in the dark."

I ran after her. "Not *that* boat—the punt. It has a motor. We can take you across and be back before anyone wakes up." I didn't know if that was true, but it seemed possible, just talking about it. I was getting excited.

"Gabe!" Ginny grabbed my arm. "Are you crazy? We can't cross the bay alone."

Delia stopped in front of me. The moonlight turned her face a pasty white. "You wouldn't have to cross the bay, not entirely," she said. "Either one of you run an outboard before?"

"I have." I didn't tell her that Uncle Paul usually started it for me, and he'd never let me run it very far from shore. But Delia didn't seem worried. She climbed to the top of a dune and held up her hand, looking across the bay. The mainland was dark and soft, like a whale resting on the surface of the water.

"Offshore wind," Delia said. "It will bring you back pretty fast. Tell you what. You take me to Murphy's Lookout—that high pile of rocks where the breakwater turns. Even at high tide, it sticks up above the water. You can land a boat there. I'll wait for the tide to turn, then walk in. By the time you're ready to leave the island, I'll be gone—unless you squeal on me again."

"We won't." I glanced at my sister to make sure she agreed, but her face was all crumpled up.

"I can't do it!" Ginny wailed. "I'll be sick!"

Delia's laugh was short and dry. "All the years I've spent on boats, you think I've never seen that? Sit in the bow, away from the engine, and you'll be fine." Delia veered to the right and headed up the beach to the little harbor as if everything were settled.

"Gabe, I can't," Ginny said again.

"You have to," I insisted. I grabbed her, holding my light so I could see her face. "Listen, you're right. I *am* scared of the dark, scared to death. I can't come back in the boat alone. And what would you say to Grandfather if I did?"

"What will *you* say to him?" Ginny demanded, but I could tell she was waffling. "You're not acting scared," she said, pulling away.

"And you're not acting seasick either," I said, "but you probably will be. Just don't throw up in my lap."

"You wish," Ginny said, but she followed me through the tall grass down to the beach. I raked my flashlight over the punt. With its oars tucked away under the seat, its motor tipped up like a duck's tail, and its anchor line stretched tight, it looked ready and waiting, eager to take us to sea.

15

On Murphy's Lookout

We stood there a minute, listening to the wind singing through the tall beach grass. Even with the moon glittering on the waves, the ocean was a deep, bottomless black. Finally Delia said briskly, "Well, who's in charge here? Every ship needs a captain." She peered up at Ginny, her hooded face barely reaching my sister's chin. "Guess we don't want our captain heaving over the side—so that leaves you, boy."

I wanted to protest that I'd never been captain of anything, but Delia was already loading her stuff into the boat. A wave hissed over the pebbles, grazing the stern. I went to the bow, beaming my light around until I found the anchor, dug it out of the sand, and brought it to the boat. I glanced at Ginny, hoping she'd tell me this was nuts, but she set her flashlight on the seat and began to coil the anchor line.

"Well, captain, what now?" Delia asked.

"Let's push her into the water," I mumbled.

"If you're going to give orders, you'll have to speak up," Delia said.

"Heave ho!" I shouted, grabbing one side of the punt.

"Gabe, you're really queer," Ginny groaned, but she took hold of the other side.

"Tide's high enough so it won't be too hard." Delia sounded almost cheery now; I guess she was glad to be leaving. She stationed herself at the bow.

"Push!" I yelled, trying to deepen my voice. I didn't feel like a captain, not one bit. My heart was pounding, and my throat was all dry. I couldn't see the breakwater, and Murphy's Lookout was completely invisible. Even the lights winking on the mainland could have been stars in outer space, they seemed so far away.

When the next wave came, we shoved the punt toward the water. It seemed heavier than the other day, probably because we didn't have Uncle Paul. We grunted and pushed, letting the waves help us; finally a big one lifted the punt off the sand. "She's afloat," Delia announced.

I gripped the bow, steadying the boat while Delia and Ginny climbed aboard. Freezing seawater poured into my boots and soaked my pants. The punt rocked and pitched. "Get in!" Ginny yelled.

My boots sloshed into deep water. I kicked my feet and tumbled over the bow into the bottom of the boat. Waves broke against the stern, nudging us back toward shore. "Push off with your oars!" Delia yelled. She shooed us toward the middle, settling herself in the stern next to the engine. "We'll start the motor when we're out of earshot."

Ginny and I wrestled with the oars, untangling them from the bottom of the boat. For once, we weren't arguing. As soon as we had them in the oarlocks, Ginny stumbled to the bow and sat down with her head on her knees.

"Ginny, come on—you can't be sick already!" I yelled over my shoulders. I dug down, but not deep enough; the oars whiffled and I got everyone wet.

"Cut it out." Ginny's voice was muffled.

"I'm not doing it on purpose!"

"Easy now," Delia said quietly. "Slow and steady." She tipped the engine into place and took my flashlight, studying the motor.

It was hard to get the feel of rowing in the dark, but finally I started pulling evenly and we rocked through the choppy breakers that filled the cove.

Delia tossed two life jackets forward. "Put these on," she said. "I hope no one needs them, but the sea's unpredictable."

We snapped the bulky jackets over our coats. "Don't you want one?" Ginny asked.

"No, I don't need it."

When Ginny and I glanced at each other nervously, Delia laughed. "Don't worry, I don't plan to drown on this boat trip."

A wave hit us sideways, rocking the punt. I grabbed the oars and started rowing again. "You could at least direct me toward the breakwater," I called to my sister.

Ginny groaned. "More to the right—I mean, pull on your left oar."

When the next wave came, we went up over the crest and down into the trough. "I'm going to be sick," Ginny warned.

"Nonsense," Delia said, "just take a few deep breaths and watch the horizon. You'll be fine." Ginny clenched her mouth tight. When we neared the mouth of the harbor, Delia said, "Now steady the oars for a minute and hold the light. We'll start the engine."

I set the oars on the gunwales and moved to the stern.

"Ever started this before?" Delia asked.

I shook my head. "Not really," I admitted.

"Well, you'll get your chance tonight. Here's the choke"—she pulled out a black knob—"and the throttle—turn it to start." I aimed the flashlight at the gearshift, making sure it was in neutral. Then Delia took the light. "Give that cord a yank—let's see if it will catch."

I hesitated. Usually, Uncle Paul pulled the cord until the engine was roaring, then he'd turn it over to me. But Delia seemed to think I could do it, so I stood up, braced my legs to keep from pitching overboard, and tugged on the cord, hard. Nothing happened. I yanked again and again. On the fifth or sixth try, the engine sputtered, then caught. Its whine was deafening; wouldn't Grandfather and Uncle Paul hear us? I quickly turned the throttle to slow the engine down.

"Stow the oars!" I yelled at Ginny. She crawled forward, staying low the way Uncle Paul had taught us, tucked the oars under the seat, and went back to the bow. I wanted to cheer. This was fun, giving my sister orders—and having her obey. I shifted into forward and grabbed the tiller. Delia moved to the middle of the punt so I could sit in the stern. The boat bucked, charging the swells. Ginny's dark form was bent over the gunwale. "Which way?" I called to her.

She peered into the darkness, motioned me toward the left, and then tucked her chin into the puffy collar of her life jacket.

"Keep an eye out!" Delia called to her.

Ginny groaned, and peered out over the bow.

"There it is!" she yelled after a few minutes, pointing dead ahead. Surf foamed where waves curled over the breakwater.

We drew up close and Delia leaned toward me. "Keep your distance!" she cried. I swerved away from the rocks, running alongside. The wind was pushing against us, and the waves seemed bigger; they crested into whitecaps like whipped cream instead of rolling in steady swells. The punt rode them like a horse taking a jump; the bow lifted for a second, then slowly dove down the back side. I liked the feel of my body plunging with the ocean, but Ginny held her hand over her mouth. The engine whined, it was working hard.

It was eerie, being out on the ocean under the moon. I was so busy trying to keep the boat pointed straight that I hardly looked at Delia until my sister shouted, "Gabe—slow down!"

I cut the engine back. Delia was leaning over the port side holding the little wooden box. As we crested the next wave, she opened the lid, and a bundle of folded letters fluttered across the top of the waves. The square papers floated for a second, very white against the dark water, before they were sucked under. Ginny twisted around, her eyes bugged out, her mouth open in a wide 0, watching the letters disappear in our wake. Without looking at either of us, Delia closed the box, stuffed it into her backpack, and shifted to the center of the boat, holding her head fixed toward the mainland as though nothing had happened.

"Why did you do that?" Ginny wailed.

Delia bent forward, cupping her hands over her mouth. "It was time."

Ginny asked something else but the wind snatched her words away; I couldn't hear her. My heart was beating in time with the throbbing of the engine. I hoped Delia didn't have any more weird tricks in her pockets.

I was relieved when the bulky black outline of Murphy's Lookout finally loomed ahead of us. Delia pointed to the place where I should land the boat: a snug, calmer patch of water behind the elbow of the breakwater. I swung the punt close to the rocks and Delia called, "Shut her down!" I cut the motor and Ginny leaned over the bow, catching a rock to hold us steady while I reached out an oar and fended us off. The boat rocked gently; Ginny and I sat close to the gunwales to keep the punt from scraping.

The lookout was wet and slick with spray. "How will you get up there?" I asked.

"Same way I always did." Delia swung her pack onto her back, then reached under her seat and brought out the milk cans. Moonlight glinted off the metal. When she looped them over her arm and started to climb out, I tugged at her sleeve, the way I used to do to my mom when I was little.

"Wait," I begged. "Why did you throw the letters away?"

She pushed her hood back so her face was stark in the moonlight. "I told you, I came out to the island to say good-bye to everyone—and that includes Jack."

"Couldn't you finish the story," Ginny said softly. "Please. We didn't tell anyone about him—and we won't, will we, Gabe?"

I shook my head. "Not unless you want us to."

Delia frowned. "Thought I told you everything earlier."

"No you didn't!" Ginny protested. "You stopped at the best part—you were planning to get married and then Jack—"

"Jilted me," Delia finished with a sigh. "Yes, you're right. Once you start a story, you're obligated to finish it, no matter how it ends." She sat down again, looking off toward the mainland. "I told you it was spring, didn't I—and the date had been set for the wedding." She paused the way Grandfather does when he's trying to get himself into the mood for a story and for a minute, I wished they could have met each other.

"I hadn't told my parents yet, but I was making

my plans," Delia went on. "Then Jack broke it off, just like that." She slashed her hand through the air. The moonlight made her eyes disappear in their dark sockets, but we could feel her cold stare. I gripped the splintery oar with both hands.

"What did he say?" Ginny whispered. I was glad she asked—I didn't quite dare.

"That he wasn't ready for marriage. Ha! What an understatement!" Delia's voice was tight, and her thin braid slipped from its pins. She sounded as if this had just happened yesterday. "He said he'd row me across," she went on. "It was late and the tide was coming in. But I sent him away, said I could make it back. When he was gone, I walked out to Murphy's and crossed to the back side where no one could see me." She pointed to the rock above us. "There was a moon, just like tonight, and the stars were clear. I threw my empty milk cans into the water. I made sure they were floating on the bay side, so people would think I'd drowned. I wanted to hurt Jack as badly as he'd hurt me, but I suppose it was my mother and father who were really sick at heart." She glared at Ginny, then at me. "Don't you ever treat *your* parents that way," she warned. "When you're young, you forget how other people might feel. By the time I was old enough to make amends, it was too late. My family was gone."

She cleared her throat. "Something broke inside

me when I left here. After I was mended, I didn't need Jack, or anyone else."

Ginny and I were completely still. I huddled into my coat. Delia's life sounded so lonesome; it made me think that even living with my prickly sister would be better than having no one at all.

"Where did you go after that?" Ginny asked.

"I disappeared. It was the end of the month; I had all the milk money. That was the only time I ever stole for keeps," she added, giving us a quick, beady stare. When we didn't say anything, she said, "I went down east to Camden, then out to Nova Scotia. I've been moving ever since, and I don't intend to stop now."

Delia buttoned her coat with her gnarled fingers and pulled up her hood. "Well, that's my story," she said. "You can take it or leave it."

Ginny's legs bounced nervously. "We believe you," she said, then blurted, "Didn't you read the letters? What did they say?"

The corner of Delia's mouth twitched. I wasn't sure if she was trying not to laugh or cry. "It was too dark to read—besides, I'm sure they were better the first time around."

"What happened to Jack?" I asked, finally finding my voice.

She gave me this surprised look. Maybe she'd forgotten I was there. Then she waved one hand at the sea. "Gone, like everyone else I knew then."

Goose bumps quivered up and down my arms. Were they all spirits now, hovering over the island?

Suddenly I remembered something. I reached in my pocket and pulled out her scarf. "Grandfather found this up in the woods," I said.

"Thanks." Delia wound the soft material around her neck. "If I've left anything else, it's too bad. This is my final farewell to Lost Island." She lifted her head until her chin was set forward. "I'm off," she said.

"Wait," Ginny begged. "The waves are so big— how will we know you've made it to shore?"

"I won't have any trouble." Maybe it was only the moonlight, but I could swear Delia's eyes were a little bit soft when she looked down at Ginny. "Tell you what, I'll leave you a sign. Just keep your eyes on the breakwater going home."

"What do you mean? What sign?" Ginny asked in a trembly voice, but Delia was on her way, and by now we both knew she didn't answer questions unless she felt like it. A swell lifted the boat and Delia gripped my shoulder with her bony hand, steadying herself as she stepped out onto the rocks, her cans clanging against each other. She stood with the surf swirling around her ankles for a second, getting her balance, then climbed slowly up the side of Murphy's Lookout to a small ledge. "Get

going now," she called, waving her hand. "Keep a
safe distance from the breakwater—you'll have the
wind at your back. I'll be gone when the tide
changes." She turned away.

"Good-bye," we called, but she didn't move.
Ginny pushed us off the rocks. As we drifted away
from the breakwater, I thought I heard Delia call
out, "Don't forget me," but I wasn't sure; the waves
made a racket as they slapped the sides of the boat.

The motor caught on the third try. I left it in
neutral a minute until it was chugging steadily.
Ginny moved to the middle seat and sat facing me.
"She didn't even say thank you!" she complained. I
turned the engine to full throttle.

I shrugged. "She's not the type!" I had to yell so
she could hear me.

Before I shifted into forward, I glanced behind
me for one last look. Delia's dark shape was silhou-
etted against the moon like a phantom. Was she
going to stand there all night? We squinted into the
darkness; Delia was motioning us away. Then she
climbed a little higher and sat down slowly, her
dark shape sinking like something filling with water;
first her skirt disappeared, then her chest and arms,
then her head, until her body seemed to melt into
the rocks.

"Do you think she'll be all right?" Ginny yelled.

I didn't have time to answer. Drifting away from

the shelter of the lookout, the pounding of surf on the rocks drowned the sputter of the engine. A wave hit us broadside and the punt dove into a deep trough.

"We've got to get going!" I yelled, revving the engine. "We'll be swamped!"

Ginny was crying. I gripped the tiller and took one last look over my shoulder. Murphy's Lookout was black and stark against the setting moon, and Delia had blended into the rocks so completely, there was no sign that she'd ever been there.

16

"The Wind's Taking Us Out to Sea!"

The wind slammed into the punt, spinning us sideways. Ginny screamed, clutching the gunwale with one hand and my arm with the other. "Do something!" she yelled.

Foam sprayed over us as we raced ahead of the waves. The engine vibrated, numbing my hand, and water splashed into the boat.

"Find the bailer!" I yelled.

"Don't boss me around!" Ginny cried, but she got down on her hands and knees, searching with her flashlight for the plastic jug. She scooped water over the gunwales, but it seemed to pour back in as fast as she bailed it out.

"Whose crazy idea was this?" She glared at me from the bottom of the boat with water streaming down her face.

I chewed on my lower lip. Even though the sky was still clear, the wind was blowing harder now. No matter which way I pointed the bow, the ocean washed in. Suddenly a wave broke right over the stern, drenching me and the engine, which started to sputter.

"Oh, no!" I gasped. I gave it full throttle, but the motor coughed, then died. I yanked the cord frantically while Ginny gripped my knees to keep me from falling overboard. The engine wouldn't even hiccup, and the smell of gasoline filled the boat.

"Let me try!" Ginny threw herself at the cord, pulling and tugging, but nothing happened. She pounded the engine with her fist. "Stupid thing!" she shouted, sinking to her knees. "What will we do?" she wailed.

I stared at her. If my sister couldn't figure this out, who could? "We'd better row," I said, fumbling for the oars. The wind rattled the hoods of our windbreakers and turned our wet jeans into hard boards.

"I hate boats!" Ginny cried, and was suddenly sick over the side.

I turned my head away, wiggling the oarlocks into place. Ginny groaned and splashed water onto her face, then huddled in the bottom of the boat with her forehead on her knees. "Ginny, you can't sit there now!" I yelled. "Look!"

She raised her head. Her face was a greenish white, and her eyes were pinched when she followed my pointing hand. The humped saddle of the island, which should have been ahead, was off to starboard.

"If we keep heading this way, we'll miss the island," I cried. "The wind's taking us out to sea!"

I turned around in my seat. Ginny scrambled up beside me, grabbed an oar, and said in a small quiet voice I'd never heard her use: "Show me what to do."

"Dig your oar into the water," I said, "this way. No, not like that—turn it when it hits the water, so it pulls—harder, Ginny, harder!"

It wasn't working. Salt from tears and spray stung my eyes so I could hardly see, but I knew we were going in circles. First Ginny's oar dug in, then mine, then a wave nudged the boat in the wrong direction. Waves splashed over the gunwales until our boots sat in pools of water.

"We're still going the wrong way!" Ginny yelled, peeking over her shoulder.

I thought of Grandfather and Uncle Paul asleep in the cabin, and our parents snug on the mainland. I thought of Cinders, curled up in his woodbox with MacDuff beside him. I wanted to see them again. I refused to end up in the cold, black water beyond Lost Island.

"We have to row at the same time," I said. "Wait, don't start yet—" I dug my oar into the water, yanking as hard as I could until the bow swung around, aimed for the island. "Now get ready, set—PULL!"

It took us a few tries to get the rhythm right. When Ginny started yelling, "PULL!" at the same time, the punt inched forward at last, moving at a slight angle to the waves.

"We're getting it!" Ginny yelled.

"Don't look," I said, gritting my teeth. "Pull!"

The wind slapped the punt until it groaned. "Pull!" We were yelling together now, doubling forward as our oars flew out of the water, then leaning back with all our strength to draw them through the sea.

We rowed and rowed and rowed. My arms burned, my stomach muscles ached, and my voice was hoarse from shouting, but I couldn't quit; if one of us stopped, the wind might turn us around. Murphy's Lookout was far away now; I wondered if Delia thought of us at all. I felt tiny compared to the enormous whooshing wind and the waves running ahead of us toward the island. We kept rowing, moving in time to our chanting. The oarlocks creaked, making their own weird music beside us. It seemed as if we rowed for hours, but each dip of the oars only moved us an inch closer.

"Pull!" we yelled, our voices getting hoarse. "Pull!"

Finally, I glanced over my shoulder and saw the bluffs at the north end of the island. Just when I thought my arms would drop from my body like dead sticks, the chopping of water against the stern quieted, then died. We were inside the cove.

"We're almost there," I whispered, "just a few more strokes."

Ginny lifted her head. To our stern, whitecaps still raced under the moon. But the swells were smooth and steady in the little harbor. We stopped rowing, drifting slowly to shore. We passed Uncle Paul's lobster boat, and I tried to imagine explaining everything to him and Grandfather.

"What will we tell them?" I wondered out loud.

"Nothing, you nerd," Ginny sighed, and then added with a giggle, "They won't ask. They'd never think *you'd* be brave enough to take a boat out in the dark, in a storm."

"Or that you'd be stupid enough." I yawned. I should have been worried, but all I could think of was Grandfather saying that Ginny and I had our *own* story to tell about Lost Island now. He was sure right!

I glanced over my shoulder. Moonlight glinted on the silvery sand of the dune. "We're here," I breathed.

Ginny scrambled to the bow and jumped out, landing in water up to her knees. "Land—I thought we'd never see it again!" she laughed, steadying the punt.

I stood up. My palms were hot and blistery. I clumped into the surf, helping Ginny drag the boat out of the waves. We weren't strong enough to haul it all the way up the beach.

"It doesn't matter—the tide's going out soon," Ginny reminded me. We wound the anchor line around a small tree, and then dug its metal spikes into the sand. My hands shook; they wouldn't do what I wanted them to.

Ginny stood close enough so she could look into my eyes. Her hair was soaked and her face was streaked. "You look like a wild man," she teased. "Your hair's sticking straight up."

"You don't look so hot yourself," I said, but we were both grinning. I wanted to hug her, but I was too embarrassed, so I punched her arm and she poked me in the ribs where she knew I was ticklish.

We stowed the oars and the life jackets and bailed out some of the water. Our teeth were chattering. I tried to hurry, but my legs wobbled; the beach seemed to lift and fall as if I were still at sea.

"Hey, Gabe," Ginny murmured, so low I had trouble hearing her, "you were really brave."

"So were you." I stood up straight and jammed

my hands in my pockets. I felt warm inside, even though my arms and legs were covered with goose bumps. I knew that sometime soon—maybe even in a few hours—I'd be mad at my sister again. She'd be bossy, I'd whine. Still, if we hadn't rowed that way, like one person fighting the wind, we might be at the bottom of the ocean now, instead of standing on the shore with soaked clothes and cold feet—alive.

But what about Delia?

Ginny looked out to sea. "What if she doesn't make it?" she whispered. She must have read my mind.

"She will. She always did before." I crossed my arms over my chest, holding myself tight. "She told us she'd wait until the tide changed. Maybe the wind will die down by morning."

"I hope so." Ginny squeezed her braid until seawater dribbled down her sleeve, then wiped her nose with her sleeve. "She won't have anyone to talk to but that awful wind."

"I guess she likes it that way." I looked behind us, then out toward the mainland. The sky was a little lighter. "Geez, Ginny, it's almost morning. We'd better get back in bed before Grandfather wakes up." I looked her right in the eye. "This time, we really won't tell them anything, right?"

"It's a deal." We shook hands with serious faces, then burst out laughing. We ran up the path to the cabin and slipped inside, gritting our teeth to keep them from chattering. MacDuff's tail thumped; I patted him and stood frozen in the middle of the room, trying to remember what to do next. Luckily, Ginny hissed, "Take your clothes off, stupid. We'll hide all the wet stuff in my pack."

We stripped to our underwear. It was light enough to see now, but I didn't care. Let Ginny look all she wanted; I was going to bed.

Ginny held out her empty pack and I shoved my clothes inside. She was shaking and her underwear was so wet I could see right through it.

"Shut up," she whispered, even though I hadn't said a word. I swallowed a laugh and stumbled into my bag, soaking up the warmth of the cozy lining. For a second, I pictured Delia's eyes as she said good-bye to us; how soft they were for an instant—and then I remembered her face at the window. She had seemed so evil and spooky then. Now she was alone on the lookout, with the waves crashing at her feet. Somehow, I knew she wouldn't be afraid—she'd just wait patiently for the tide to turn around. She's brave, I thought, and then I grinned to myself in the dark. *She's* brave—and I am, too. She taught me that.

Thanks, Delia, I thought. In the next instant, I was asleep.

17

Delia's Gone

I woke up with Uncle Paul's hand shaking my shoulder. "Wake up, Gabe; rise and shine, Ginny— I've never seen you two so dead to the world."

I groaned and ducked my head deeper into my bag. It felt as if we'd only been asleep for ten minutes. Every inch of my body was cramped and sore. Ginny whimpered when Uncle Paul said, "Come on, kids—you've had plenty of hours in the sack. We all overslept this morning, even your grandfather. We need to get you home."

I sat up. Sunshine poured into the room; my eyes didn't seem to be working and it was a minute before I could focus. The top of Ginny's head poked out of her bag like a caterpillar inside its cocoon. Uncle Paul laughed, shaking his head. "Guess we worked you too hard yesterday." His cheeks were red and his eyes were bright; he must have been outdoors already.

I started to look for my clothes so I wouldn't have to meet his eyes. It was going to be hard, hiding something from him and Grandfather all day—or at least until we were sure Delia had made it safely to shore.

"When's low tide?" I yawned, trying to sound casual.

Uncle Paul checked his watch. "Should be about now."

Ginny sat up suddenly. "Are we going right home?"

Uncle Paul nodded. "Soon as we get the boat loaded. I got a start on it already; we'll take off as soon as you've had breakfast."

"Aren't we going to look for Delia some more?" Ginny asked. I was impressed by how innocent she sounded, as if nothing had happened last night. I ducked my chin so I wouldn't give anything away.

"I don't think so." Uncle Paul rubbed his head until his bristly hair stood up like a kid with a punk haircut. He lowered his voice. "Your grandfather wants to bring out a search party. But just between you and me, I'm going to try to talk him out of it. I have a hunch Delia can take care of herself. What do you think?"

"Uh—sure," I said, glancing at Ginny. She lowered her eyes. "I mean, she got out here all right," I mumbled. "Besides, she told us she wouldn't stay long." And she'd better be across the breakwater by now, I thought, or she's done for.

Uncle Paul grunted, stepped out on the porch, and came right back with the lamb. Cinders bleated when he saw me.

"Thinks you're his mama," Uncle Paul laughed. "He needs one last bottle before we leave. You kids eat up quickly now; your grandfather's ready to go and you know how he gets when he has to wait."

The lamb nuzzled my face. "Hey, there's no milk there," I protested, pushing him gently away. Ginny and I got dressed quickly, glad it was warm enough for shorts. There'd be no way to explain our wet clothes from last night.

We fed the lamb and packed all our dry stuff in my pack, leaving the wet things in Ginny's. I snatched bites from a stale bagel, but I wasn't really hungry and Ginny refused to eat. "I'll only lose it on the boat," she said.

"You did okay last night," I reminded her, but she poked me; Grandfather was on the porch. He limped when he came in and his blue eyes snapped. "Time to go, kids."

Ginny and I hoisted our packs while Uncle Paul and Grandfather closed up the cabin and padlocked the door.

We walked in a line down the hill. Cinders looked tiny tucked under Uncle Paul's arm. As soon as we could see the ocean, I glanced quickly toward the breakwater, but there was no sign of Delia; Murphy's Lookout loomed high above the wet stones, sparkling in the sun. We passed the old cellar hole, which looked small and jumbled in the daylight. The little birch tree growing up from the floor rustled in the wind. Was it all a dream?

As we came over the big dune near the cove, we saw the white plume of MacDuff's tail waving near the place where we'd anchored the boat. The punt was halfway into the water now, filled with our stuff, and the engine was tipped up just the way we'd left it. "Come on, Duffer," I said, but MacDuff kept his nose to the ground; he growled, then whined.

Grandfather glanced at Uncle Paul. "The dog's been snuffling around in there ever since we came down." His voice sounded tired. "I think that woman must have tried to take the boat. I could swear I left it anchored higher up on the beach—though I can't be sure, now the tide's out. I guess it'd be too heavy for her to move alone."

He turned to me, his blue eyes sharp under his shaggy eyebrows. "You kids are awfully quiet this morning—something wrong?"

"Uh-uh," I said, shaking my head, and Ginny added quickly, "We're just tired after yesterday."

Grandfather grunted. "Well, it *was* a long day. Guess us old folks have more stamina than the young ones, eh, Paul? Come on, let's finish loading up."

Whew, I thought, another close one. I thought we were safe but then Uncle Paul said, "All this gear—let's use the engine, Pop."

Grandfather kicked up sand with his boot. "The darned thing's flooded. We'll have to row. It doesn't take long when the sea's this calm."

My face felt hot. I set my bags on the beach and pretended to look for interesting stones while Grandfather and Uncle Paul discussed the best way to ferry the stuff to the lobster boat.

It took us three trips to move everything, and every time Grandfather came back to shore, he looked up and down the beach; I guess he hoped Delia might show up.

Ginny wouldn't get in until the last trip out. Uncle Paul had started the engine on the big boat; it rumbled and sputtered while we climbed into the punt. I held the lamb tight in my arms and MacDuff sat at my feet.

"Things will be more peaceful on our next visit," Grandfather said, shoving us off. I caught Ginny's eyes, and this time, neither one of us could keep from grinning. If Grandfather only knew!

Luckily, Grandfather didn't ask me to take the

oars; my hands were blistered and raw from last night. I kept them hidden in Cinder's soft fleece while Grandfather rowed steadily, watching the island with his cap pushed up high on his forehead.

"If that woman is Delia Simpson, like you say, I don't suppose we'll ever find her," he said suddenly. "She must know this island backward and forward."

I nodded and gave him a weak smile. It was nice that he believed me a little bit, but as far as I was concerned, the less talk about Delia, the better.

We came alongside the lobster boat and hoisted the last of our gear up to Uncle Paul. When everyone was aboard, we lashed the punt's long rope to a cleat at the stern. Grandfather pulled up the anchor and we chugged forward out of the cove.

Ginny settled herself at the stern. She looked green already, but I didn't feel like teasing her, not after last night.

"Gabriel!" Uncle Paul shouted over the drone of the motor. I went forward into the half-cabin where he stood at the wheel. He pointed to a waterproof metal box on the floor. "Take the field glasses. Maybe you'll catch sight of your old woman as we pull away."

I snapped the box open, looped the strap of the binoculars over my neck, and walked carefully to the stern, letting my feet roll with the rocking of the boat. The smell of diesel fuel mixed with the wet scent of lanolin from the wool bags. I was glad my stomach was strong. Ginny was squinting straight ahead; at first I thought she was trying not to be sick, but then I realized she was looking at the breakwater.

I put the field glasses to my eyes, searching the island first so Uncle Paul wouldn't suspect anything. I twisted the knobs until the cabin came into focus, then the shearing pens and the flagpole. I swooped the binoculars from one end of Lost Island to the other, saying good-bye to the grapevine house, the big meadow, the shearing pens—even the little graveyard. When I found the tiny headstones leaning toward the water, I felt bad that Delia hadn't had time to clean up her parents' graves. Maybe next time I'd be brave enough to do that for her—maybe.

We came out of the sheltered cove. The breakwater stretched to our left and I aimed the field glasses toward the line of rocks. At first, the slow swells made it hard to hold the binoculars steady. Ginny beckoned to me; I leaned over and she cupped her hand to my ear. "See anything?" she asked. I shook my head but I kept looking.

We steamed across the bay. Uncle Paul's legs were braced in a wide stance; he kept one hand on the wheel and the other on Grandfather's arm, shouting at him over the steady thrumming of the engine. I couldn't hear what they were saying. Grandfather shook his head, then shrugged his shoulders. Maybe Uncle Paul was talking him out of the search party idea.

When Murphy's Lookout came in sight, my palms felt sweaty and I looked back at Lost Island. Even in the daylight, it seemed like a long way to row, and the ocean beyond stretched out forever. I leaned over to my sister. "We were crazy last night," I said.

Her face was pinched from so much squinting. "What about that sign Delia was supposed to leave us?" she asked.

The sign. I'd almost forgotten. As we passed the lookout, I peered through the binoculars again, checking the stone tower. Nothing there, and the breakwater was still empty. I was about to give up when I spotted something bright. My hands shook. A silver flash glinted in the sunlight, and I knew what it was even before the rocks came into sharp focus, showing me every jagged line. The binoculars were so powerful, I felt as if I could step right off the boat onto the wall. And if I just reached out my hand, I could pick up the two silver milk cans, pitching from side to side in the waves.

I looked around quickly. Grandfather sat on a wool bag, his cap pulled over his eyes, his hand on

MacDuff's shiny coat. Ginny's head was bent over her knees. I tapped her on the shoulder. Her eyes were glassy. "Go away," she groaned, "I feel awful."

"Look." I shoved the field glasses into her hands. "In the water, right below the lookout—" I guided the glasses with my hand.

She swallowed hard, then squinted into them, adjusting the focus. "I don't see anything," she complained, but then she gasped, "Oh *no!*"

"Quiet," I warned her. We huddled together. Ginny clutched my arm and I didn't push her away. My heart was pounding. The milk cans rode the waves in and out; even though we couldn't hear anything over the beat of the engine, I could imagine how they'd clang against the rocks. I glanced at Uncle Paul, but he was watching the little blips on his radar screen and Grandfather seemed to be dozing.

"Gabe!" Ginny gripped me even tighter. "Do you think she drowned this time?"

"I don't know," I whispered. Something was wrong with *my* stomach now.

We watched the breakwater. I knew what it was like, walking on those stones at low tide. Rockweed covers everything, making a spongy mat that can slip right out from under you. Delia was old; she could easily have fallen, dropping the cans.

I took a deep breath, forcing myself to take another look through the glasses. The breakwater was empty, and the ocean was bright and smooth. I thought of everything Delia had told us and suddenly, I knew what she had done.

I closed my eyes and pictured the sun rising slowly, waking Delia where she dozed high above the breakwater. As the jagged rocks finally emerged from the sea, she'd climb carefully down from her perch. Balancing on a flat stone, she'd take one milk can and fling it into the water; then she'd heave the second one, waiting for the splash before beginning her last slow walk into shore. I could imagine her taking one final look at the island before she disappeared forever. And as if she were standing right beside me, I heard her voice, repeating what she'd told us last night: *I made sure they were floating on the bay side, so people would think I'd drowned.* I smiled. She was a crafty old lady, that's for sure.

Ginny tugged my arm. Her eyes were red. "What's so funny? Don't you realize she might be dead?" she demanded.

"I think she's okay." I talked right into her ear, keeping an eye on Grandfather and Uncle Paul. "She was probably trying to fool Grandfather, just like she did Jack sixty years ago."

"But the cans don't tell us she's safe, do they?"

Ginny wiped her eyes, and I didn't say anything. Uncle Paul turned the boat away from the breakwater and headed up the coastline toward Stone Harbor where Mom and Dad would meet us. The waves came at us sideways and Ginny groaned, dropping her head in her lap. The breakwater was off to our stern now; when I peered through the field glasses one last time, I nearly cried aloud.

"Ginny!" I hissed, poking her with my elbow. "I found it!"

She grabbed the binoculars and I watched her face break into a smile. With my bare eyes I could see the tall iron spike in the sand that marked the beginning of the breakwater, and on top, something gauzy fluttered in the wind, a scarlet flag celebrating the new day. Even at this distance, I knew it was Delia's scarf.

"She made it," Ginny whispered. She lowered the field glasses, squinting as the breakwater slowly slipped away behind us. Her eyes were shining and her cheeks were pink again. "We saved her, Gabe, we really did it."

"Delia saved herself," I said, but I hugged my arms across my chest and stood up, letting my legs roll with the swells until I felt as if I were dancing with the ocean.

Ginny stood beside me in the stern, and we

watched the breakwater dissolve into a distant black line. Waves slapped the boat, beating like the song I heard in my head. *Delia's gone*, it sang, keeping time with the steady thump of the waves and hum of the motor. *Delia's gone, one more round, Delia's gone.*

Glossary

belly wool: the wool from the sheep's belly, usually discarded because it's dirty.

Border collie: a medium-sized, black or brown farm dog, with white markings, used for herding sheep.

colostrum: special milk produced by a mammal during the first few days of her baby's life. It is very high in protein, vitamins, and minerals and helps protect the newborn against diseases, as well as giving it strength after the birth.

culls: sheep that are separated out of a flock, usually because they are sick, old, or have problems.

ewe: a female sheep.

fleece: a sheep's wool coat.

generator: a machine that makes electricity, using mechanical energy.

gunwale (pronounced "gunnel"): the upper edge of a boat's side.

lanolin: a yellowish-white greasy substance found in sheep's wool and used to make ointments and creams.

port: the left side of a boat or ship.

punt: a small boat, usually with an outboard motor, used by Maine lobstermen for fishing or for traveling to and from their lobster boats at their moorings.

ram: a male sheep.

shearing: removing fleece or hair, using hand or electric clippers.

skirting: separating the dirty tags and belly wool from the fleece; also, picking out twigs, sticks, and grass to clean it.

starboard: the right side of a boat or ship.

tags: the dirty wool from a sheep's neck and hind end.

wool tower: a tall wooden frame, built to hold the long burlap sacks that the shepherd stores his wool in.

Dog Commands

"**Come by**": Sweep around to the left.
"**Way to me**": Sweep around to the right.
"**Walk in**": Bring the sheep toward me.
"**Way round**": Go out beyond the flock.
"**Git *down*!**": Crouch and hold the sheep.